Bolan knew he had to act fast

Weapons carry was always a balance between speed and conceal ability; the more concealed a gun was the slower it was to bring into action. The .380 was in his pocket by necessity, and drawing it would be slow.

Deathly slow.

And Wilson's Black Widow—wherever it was—was likely to be just as tardy.

The FARC men had all drawn their weapons and were waiting to shoot all three of Marquez's guests if necessary. And while he didn't bother looking behind him, Bolan suspected the deaf giant had drawn a weapon of some kind, as well.

Bolan was fast and accurate. But considering the lopsided odds in both numbers and firepower, he wasn't going to make it out of this gunfight alive. Wilson would try his best to help, Bolan knew.

But the retired Texas Ranger would die trying—just like the Executioner.

MACK BOLAN ®
The Executioner

The Executioner®
Don Pendleton's

TROPIC BLAST

A GOLD EAGLE BOOK FROM
WORLDWIDE®

TORONTO • NEW YORK • LONDON
AMSTERDAM • PARIS • SYDNEY • HAMBURG
STOCKHOLM • ATHENS • TOKYO • MILAN
MADRID • WARSAW • BUDAPEST • AUCKLAND

First edition December 2006
ISBN-13: 978-0-373-64337-0
ISBN-10:   0-373-64337-3

Special thanks and acknowledgment to
Jerry VanCook for his contribution to this work.

TROPIC BLAST

Go into emptiness, strike voids, bypass what he
defends, hit him where he does not expect you.
                                    —*Ts'as Ts'ao*, 155–220 A.D.

I will hunt my enemy and infiltrate his territory. I
will catch him by surprise. He won't see me coming.
                                    —Mack Bolan

THE
MACK BOLAN
LEGEND

Nothing less than a war could have fashioned the destiny of the man called Mack Bolan. Bolan earned the Executioner title in the jungle hell of Vietnam.

But this soldier also wore another name—Sergeant Mercy. He was so tagged because of the compassion he showed to wounded comrades-in-arms and Vietnamese civilians.

Mack Bolan's second tour of duty ended prematurely when he was given emergency leave to return home and bury his family, victims of the Mob. Then he declared a one-man war against the Mafia.

He confronted the Families head-on from coast to coast, and soon a hope of victory began to appear. But Bolan had broken society's every rule. That same society started gunning for this elusive warrior—to no avail.

So Bolan was offered amnesty to work within the system against terrorism. This time, as an employee of Uncle Sam, Bolan became Colonel John Phoenix. With a command center at Stony Man Farm in Virginia, he and his new allies—Able Team and Phoenix Force—waged relentless war on a new adversary: the KGB.

But when his one true love, April Rose, died at the hands of the Soviet terror machine, Bolan severed all ties with Establishment authority.

Now, after a lengthy lone-wolf struggle and much soul-searching, the Executioner has agreed to enter an "arm's-length" alliance with his government once more, reserving the right to pursue personal missions in his Everlasting War.

1

Mack Bolan watched his old friend and longtime pilot Jack Grimaldi manipulate the controls of the Learjet as the plane began its descent over Bogotá, Colombia. Grimaldi had to have felt the look, because he turned in his seat. The pilot's eyebrows lowered and his lips turned down slightly. "Something bothering you, Sarge?" he asked.

"Uh-huh," the big man said.

"What is it?" Grimaldi asked.

"I don't know…yet," Bolan replied.

Grimaldi nodded and turned back to the controls in front of him. He had been through too many wars with the Executioner to question his friend's instincts.

Bolan unbuckled his seat belt and moved between the seats, making his way quickly past the canvas equipment bags he had ready to unload as soon as they touched down. Near the rear of the plane, he stopped in front of one of the lockers bolted to the wall. He twisted the latch, reached in and pulled out what he needed. A moment later, he was in his seat again and pulling the visor down in front of him.

As he flipped up the cover hiding the mirror, Grimaldi said, "Looks like you're ready for action." The pilot chuckled under his breath. "That'll be a nice shade on you."

"Glad you like it," Bolan said as he went to work in the mirror. "I'll let you wear it when I'm finished with it."

"I'll stick with the way I look now, if you don't mind," Grimaldi said, tapping the bill to his suede Alaskan bush pilot cap. "God didn't give me much, but I'm satisfied."

Bolan continued his preparation, glancing at his friend out of the corner of his eye.

"Wilson meeting you on the ground?" Grimaldi asked as they descended.

"Yeah," Bolan said. "Drove up from Peru last night." The Executioner thought briefly of the retired Texas Ranger now living in Colombia's neighboring country. Wilson had been one of the law-enforcement personnel singled out for specialized training at Stony Man Farm, the covert agency with whom Bolan had an arm's length working relationship. Like other men chosen for this top training, Wilson had arrived at Stony Man Farm blindfolded, gone through the various courses of instruction, then left the Farm blindfolded, to return to Texas. Known simply as "blacksuits" because of the stretchy, skintight combat uniforms they wore, the Farm followed their graduates' careers from then on, even into retirement. Hal Brognola, Stony Man's Director of Sensitive Operations—and another long-time friend of the Executioner's—never knew when one of them might come in handy.

This had been one of those times.

Bolan finished with the mirror and flipped the visor back up. Everything was going according to plan so far. But the feeling that violence was imminent had grown even stronger.

Grimaldi set down the Learjet's wheels on the ground

and the plane raced across the tarmac, gradually slowing as a Colombian customs vehicle appeared at the end of the runway. Because of the nature of the Executioner's mission, and he would have to enter the country like anyone else—clearing customs and open to a complete search of both his person and the private plane should the whims of the officials take that course. If they did, trouble would be imminent.

In addition to the sound-suppressed Beretta 93-R in his shoulder rig and the .44 Magnum Desert Eagle on his hip, the bags behind his seat were filled with other weapons, extra magazines and ammunition.

But as the world's premier exporter of illegal drugs, few Colombians were concerned about what came *into* the country. And both Bolan and Brognola knew that a little money stuffed into the right hands at the airport would likely be the only necessary documentation.

They were right.

An overweight, uniformed man holding a clipboard walked forward as Bolan exited the plane. Speaking in Spanish, he asked to see the Learjet's papers as well as both Bolan's and Grimaldi's passports. Handing the requested papers to the man, he waited as the Colombian rifled quickly through them. Only a quick and practiced eye would have noticed the man's hand as he pocketed the money stuck between the passports.

The man nodded, turned and headed back toward the terminal.

Bolan turned back to the open door of the cockpit. As he did, he caught a quick glimpse of another man, dressed in faded green army fatigues, a khaki T-shirt, and a floppy green boonie cap that hid most of his face, walking across the tarmac toward the plane.

It took a second for Bolan to recognize Wilson. The man had lost some of the muscle mass he'd had when he'd been a regular in the Texas Ranger weight room before retiring. But the major difference was the clothing. Bolan realized that except for when the man wore a blacksuit, he had never seen Wilson in anything except cowboy boots, his four-piece silver Texas Ranger duty belt buckle, and the official white Ranger hat with the gold captain's star concho band.

In retirement, it looked as if the Texan had traded in his boots and hat and gone native. It took two looks and a frown for Wilson to recognize Bolan. But when he did, he smiled the same friendly smile Bolan remembered.

Neither man, however, had time to speculate or comment on the other's change in appearance. Before Bolan could reach out to shake Wilson's hand, a stream of steady automatic riflefire suddenly crackled over the other noises of the airport, and a series of holes appeared in the skin of the Learjet.

"Take off, Jack!" the Executioner shouted over his shoulder as he and Wilson hit the tarmac.

"Your gear bags, Sarge!" Grimaldi shouted, starting to rise from his seat behind the controls to throw them down.

"Forget them!" Bolan shouted. "There's no time. Get out of here, *now!*" The gunfire, Bolan knew, would far supercede the leniency his money had bought from the Colombian customs man. And if the Learjet was still on the ground when the shooting stopped, it would be searched from top to bottom. If that happened, they were in for serious problems. It made more sense to enter the country with nothing but the weapons he had on him and pick up whatever else he might need along the way.

Two more bursts of fire came at the downed men from two different directions. Bolan realized there were at least *three* gunmen trying to kill them. He rolled quickly to his side, reaching under his jacket and jerking the Desert Eagle from the belt-slide holster on his hip. Behind him, Grimaldi spun the Learjet through a fast U-turn on the ground. As he rolled the other way, the Beretta 93-R was in the Executioner's other hand in a split second. In his peripheral vision he saw that Wilson, had drawn what looked like a pair of highly engraved and decorated 1911 Government Model .45s from somewhere beneath his jungle clothing.

Both men waited as another round of fire passed over their heads, then the Executioner yelled, "Right!" Like synchronized swimmers, both men rolled.

The next volleys of fire tore rivets through the ground in the exact spots where Bolan and Wilson had been a moment earlier.

Bolan was able to pinpoint at least one of the shooters. Perhaps fifty yards away, he saw a dark-skinned man wearing a bright yellow *guayabera* shirt, the stock of an M-16 pressed to his shoulder. Taking careful aim with the Desert Eagle, the Executioner lined up the front and rear sights and squeezed the trigger.

A mammoth, 240-grain semijacked hollowpoint round blasted from the Eagle's beak to spin through the upper center of the yellow shirt. As the rifleman's heart exploded, the M-16 fell from his hands.

Bolan heard Wilson fire twice from where he lay next to him, and saw one of the decorative .45s buck in the former Ranger's hand. Letting his eyes follow the angle of the pistol barrel, the Executioner spotted another gunner half-hiding behind a two-seat Cessna next to the hangars to his left. Wilson's rounds hit the man in the shoulder, causing him to drop his assault rifle.

Bolan triggered his Beretta and a 3-round burst spit quietly from the barrel. Two of the subsonic rounds caught Wilson's target in the throat and face, sending him to hell a half-second behind the man wearing the yellow shirt.

But the shooting was far from over.

More autofire ripped around them as Bolan yelled out again. "Paul!" he shouted over the explosions. "We're sitting ducks out here! We've got to move!"

"No argument from me!" the Texas Ranger drawled.

"Left!" Bolan yelled, and the two men rolled in unison once again, barely evading more rifle rounds. As he rolled, the Executioner took in the surroundings behind him. He saw nothing that would serve either as cover or concealment. They were on the edge of the airport, in the area reserved for small private craft, and nothing but open ground lay behind them for a good two hundred yards to the perimeter fence.

Rolling to a halt, the Executioner spied a long-haired man with another M-16 and tapped the trigger of the Desert Eagle again. A 240-grain hollowpoint round hit the rifleman's skull, disintegrating the bone and taking the entire left side of his face with it as it bored through and out the back of his head.

The gunfire continued. Bolan could tell the assault was all coming from one general area—a parking lot roughly a hundred yards away, near the terminal. Scattered behind and between the parked vehicles, he saw close to a dozen men.

All were armed with the same M-16s as their downed comrades.

"There's no place to hide!" Bolan shouted as the Beretta coughed out another quiet burst. "We're going to have to take the fight *to them!*"

"Well," Wilson drawled as a round struck the ground an inch from his face, "ain't no time like the present, if you're askin' me!"

Bolan and the retired Ranger rose to their feet amid the ongoing flurry of fire. For a moment, rifle rounds exploded all around them—at their feet, over their heads, to their sides. Whether it was poor marksmanship on the part of the shooters or good luck on the part of Bolan and Wilson, none of the rounds found their mark.

The firefight suddenly died down as the two men did the *unthinkable*—running toward their assailants rather than away from them.

The men with the M-16s halted their fire in wonderment for a few seconds. That gave Bolan and Wilson time to clear half of the open ground between them.

As he sprinted forward, the Executioner heard Wilson cut loose with a loud rebel yell at his side. Both men triggered their weapons as they ran, keeping up a steady hail of cover fire as they neared their attackers.

Bolan watched three of the shooters in the parking lot fall as he and Wilson raced forward. Twenty-five yards from the parking lot, Bolan knew they had pressed their luck as far as they dared. From that distance, a blind man had a good chance of hitting them with a rifle. "Down and roll!" he shouted.

Wilson did as instructed. Both men fell forward into shoulder rolls, evading sudden burst of .223 fire before rolling back to their feet, still firing. They covered the last few feet to the closest cars in the parking lot as more rounds zipped over their heads.

"Take cover!" the Executioner ordered, and a moment later both he and Wilson were below the engine blocks of adjacent vehicles.

The riflefire stopped as soon as they'd dropped out of sight. In the distance, they could hear the screams of approaching police sirens. He knew if he and Wilson were still there when the oncoming officials arrived, they'd be taken into custody.

As his mind raced for a plan of action, the men with the rifles gave it to him. Evidently as concerned about the oncoming sirens as the Executioner, they suddenly ducked into several of the parked cars. Bolan heard the engines roar as keys were twisted in the ignitions.

Rising slightly from behind his cover vehicle, Bolan saw a yellow taxicab that had stopped at the edge of the parking lot. He remembered seeing it slowly roll that way just before the first rounds of fire had broken out. The cabbie appeared to have frozen in fear behind the wheel, not certain whether he should back up, drive forward, or stay where he was.

"Follow me!" the Executioner called out as the cars carrying the shooters began squealing their tires out of the parking lot. Bolan rose to his feet and sprinted through the stationary vehicles, looking like a tailback evading tacklers as he threaded his way toward the cab. Behind him, he could hear Wilson's pounding feet.

When he reached the taxi, the Executioner ripped open the door, grabbed the cabdriver by the arm and jerked him out onto the pavement. The man was too frightened to make any sound whatsoever.

Wilson didn't have to be told what to do next. As

Bolan slid behind the wheel, the retired Ranger dropped in on the other side of the cab to ride shotgun.

The Executioner spun the tires of the cab out of the lot in pursuit of the fleeing riflemen just as several police cars—sirens screaming and lights flashing—reached the scene. They were close enough that Bolan could see the insignias of the airport police on the doors. Twisting the wheel at the last second to avoid a head-on collision with one of the vehicles, he took off after his prey.

One thing was obvious. The leak he'd been warned about was real. Outside of the personnel at Stony Man Farm, the only two men who should have known about his arrival in Columbia were the presidents of Colombia and the United States.

Bolan drove the cab over a curb and took off down the street, his mind racing with the ongoing chase and the mission that had brought him to Colombia in the first place. Carlos Gomez-Garcia, or "Pepe 88" as he was currently called, was the leader of the 28th Front, a division of the narcoterrorist FARC organization. And just as he had so many times in the past before the army or police raided his ranch in the country's high jungle, he had somehow received advance warning. This time an American was coming. He had sent men to the airport to kill Bolan before he ever got started.

And he had come within a hairbreadth of doing just that.

Bolan twisted the steering wheel, screeching the cab's tires around a corner as they left the airport and clearing his mind of everything except the situation at hand. There would be time to look at the big picture later. At the moment, he had more immediate problems.

Pepe 88's men were ahead of him and Wilson, and three Colombian airport police cars raced after them.

And both parties would happily kill the Executioner and the former Texas Ranger.

2

The last car in the fleeing line of FARC vehicles was a Pontiac Bonneville. Bolan chased it, and the rest of the vehicles ahead of it, from the airport toward Bogotá. Every few seconds an arm appeared holding a shining stainless-steel revolver, fired two-to-three shots, then disappeared again inside the vehicle.

The Executioner swerved the cab each time to avoid the onslaught of lead, often coming within inches of a head-on collision with oncoming traffic.

So far, the airport police had been content to utilize only their lights and sirens. But the Executioner suspected that before they hit the heavily populated city, shots would be fired from the rear as well. He knew he had to do something to keep that from happening—something that would put an end to the police pursuit without injuring the cops themselves.

"Take the wheel," he ordered Wilson, next to him.

The former blacksuit didn't have to ask why. He knew what Bolan had planned and, reaching across the cab, he grabbed the steering wheel.

Bolan pressed the button, rolling down the window next to him. Twisting in his seat, he drew the Desert Eagle from the belt-slide holster on his hip. He adjusted the side mirror slightly until the police car racing directly behind them was in full view.

The loud wail of the sirens pierced his ears. Blue and red lights flashed across the reflective glass.

With his foot still pressing down on the accelerator, the Executioner reached across his chest and rested his forearm on the door. Aiming the muzzle of the Desert Eagle rearward, he rested his thumb lightly on the trigger. With his left hand he reached up and flipped the safety off. Then, lining up the sights in the mirror, he dropped them on the left front tire of the lead airport police car and pressed his thumb forward.

The big .44 Magnum gun exploded with a deafening roar inside the cab, causing Wilson to curse under his breath. The odd grip Bolan had been forced to take on the weapon—a grip for which no handgun had been designed—magnified the recoil, making the hand cannon jump high in his hand.

Bolan knew his sights had been well aligned but, as the bullet left the barrel, the cab hit a pothole in the road. The shot jerked high. The left front headlight of the police car behind them shattered. But the pursuit continued.

Taking a deep breath, Bolan lined up the sights again. He was about to trigger another shot at the tire when Wilson roared, "Look out!" and twisted the steering wheel violently to the right.

Bolan was thrown hard against the door as two quick explosions sounded in succession in front of the cab. He looked up just in time to see the arm holding the revolver disappear into the Pontiac again.

For the third time the Executioner lined the sights up in the mirror. Holding the Desert Eagle as steady as he could on the bumpy road, he took another breath and let half of it out. Slowly, his thumb moved forward on the trigger. But this time the cab hit a bump and jerked upward, triggering the shot before he was ready. In the mirror, he saw sparks ignite on the road to the left of the wailing airport police car.

"This is getting us nowhere," Bolan said in disgust, looking forward again to see the city growing closer. Behind him, he heard muffled explosions as the airport police returned his shots. With lead flying at the cab from both front and back, he asked, "Can you reach the accelerator?"

"Yeah," Wilson said, nodding. He stretch his leg and turned sideways in his seat as Bolan pulled his foot off the pedal.

Pulling his knees up onto the driver's seat, the Executioner reached down and strapped the seat belt across the back of his calves.

"I remember this training," Wilson said with a short chuckle. "Thought I'd *never* get the hang of it at first."

Bolan didn't answer. He stuck his head out the window, only to pull it back in as a shot from the police vehicle struck the roof of the cab. Almost simultaneously, Wilson swerved again to avoid new rounds from the FARC car in front. His face hardening in determination, the Executioner leaned out of the window once more.

With his stomach resting on the bottom of the open window, Bolan raised the Desert Eagle in both hands. He let the front sight fall between the two posts at the rear. But this time he was facing the oncoming police, with his index finger rather than his thumb on the trigger. And there was no mirror to distort the sight picture in front of his eyes.

Bolan's trigger finger eased back on the hard steel.

A second later, the Desert Eagle, then the left front tire of the police car, exploded.

The Executioner pulled himself back into the car and grabbed the wheel. Wilson really did remember his training and unbuckled Bolan's seat belt from across his calves at the same time. The former blacksuit stayed sitting sideways, his gaze glued to the road ahead as Bolan looked into the rearview mirror.

The Executioner watched the lead airport police car slide and fishtail down the road behind them. Cars in the oncoming lane quickly pulled onto the shoulder to avoid being hit. The police vehicle slowed quickly, and the one just behind it crashed into the bumper, locking the two cars together. They finally ground to a halt in the middle of the road. Bolan saw the uniformed cops getting out of the cars as the third airport police vehicle slowed behind them.

No one appeared to be hurt as the men in the third car got out to check on their comrades. Bolan chuckled quietly to himself. There was plenty of room for the third car to get around the two that had wrecked. But the officers were using the safety of their brothers as an excuse not to pursue the cab or the FARC vehicles alone. Bolan couldn't blame them.

They had reached the outskirts of Bogotá, and had begun passing isolated buildings, small fruit stands, and the occasional gas station. Intersecting roads appeared on both sides of the two-lane road to the airport but the flashing lights, sirens, and explosions of gunfire had stopped most. The cab had slowed as the Executioner took out the tire behind him, and the Pontiac and other FARC vehicles were close to a hundred yards ahead. But the road between them was clear.

No one who wasn't already involved in the melee wanted to join it.

Bolan floored the accelerator, and the cab's engine coughed and burped. The Executioner tightened his fists around the steering wheel, wishing he had a more powerful vehicle at his disposal. But the thought flew out of his head as quickly as it had entered. All of the wishing in the world wasn't going to change his taxicab into a race car.

But as they continued to draw closer to the city proper, the gap between the cab and the FARC vehicles grew smaller. Bolan knew that was more because of the congested traffic ahead than the speed of the taxi. If he could just hold on—not lose any more ground—he'd eventually catch up to the men who had tried to kill him and Wilson at the airport.

The Executioner's mind sped far faster than the cab he drove. If possible, he needed to take at least one of the men alive. They would all be lower echelon shooters in Pepe 88's organization. But they still might be able to provide enough information to get him started.

The arm that had shot at them earlier had quit when they'd achieved their present distance. That told Bolan that the men in the cars had given up their plan to kill him, and were looking to simply escape themselves. He pushed the cab onward. Catching them would be a matter of patience.

Gradually, the gap between the cab and Pontiac closed. At the same time, the buildings and other small businesses to the sides of the highway grew thicker, and soon Bolan and Wilson found themselves passing street signs. They had traveled far enough from the scene of the wreck and the gunfire that the drivers around them were not aware of the hostilities. And that ignorance brought on the courage to merge in front of the cab. A late-model Chevrolet and a broken down Ford pickup drifted between the taxi and the FARC vehicles.

Bolan floored the accelerator and pulled out into the oncoming lane, passing the pickup with just enough time to avoid being hit by a tractor-trailer truck heading out of the city. But when he tried the same thing with the Chevy, he was forced back behind the car as a string of vehicles rushed past.

Momentarily stalled, the Executioner watched as Wilson shoved fresh magazines into the grips of his twin .45s. Then Wilson took the wheel as Bolan reloaded the Beretta and Desert Eagle.

Ahead, two more cars wedged in between the cab and the Pontiac. The Executioner tried to pass the Chevy again. But again he was forced back. He looked to the right-hand shoulder. There was plenty of room there to race past the cars in front of him. The problem was that the people of Bogotá seemed to regard that area as a sidewalk and set up fruit and vegetable stands right next to the highway. The traffic was too thick to see ahead far enough to be sure that he wouldn't run down innocent people by taking that path.

The Executioner took a deep breath. Frustration never did anyone any good. But he knew it could do much harm so he refused to allow such an emotion into his heart or brain. They would either catch up to the FARC shooters, or they wouldn't. And if they didn't, he'd come up with another plan to destroy Pepe 88 and his narcoterrorists.

A few minutes later, the Pontiac suddenly turned onto a side road while the two cars ahead of it—a big blue Suburban followed by a compact Nissan Pathfinder—drove on. Then, almost immediately, the Suburban turned right while the Nissan turned left.

Traffic was too thick for Bolan to even see the vehicles, let alone keep up with them. And when he looked down at the gasoline gauge Bolan saw that they were riding on empty.

Like it or not, this pursuit was over.

Fearful that by now the police had put the cab's description out over the airwaves, the Executioner turned off the big thoroughfare himself. He kept the taxi well below the speed limit as he drove, slowing even further when he saw a theater. Though it was only midafternoon—and siesta time at that—some event had to be going on inside because the parking lot was full.

Bolan pulled the cab into the parking lot, then into a space between two large SUVs. The vehicles were big enough to at least partially hide the taxi, and would do so at least as long as whatever was going on in the theater continued.

Turning to Wilson, Bolan said, "Grab our gear, I'll hook us up with some wheels that aren't so hot."

Wilson nodded as he began gathering up empty pistol magazines from the seats and floor of the cab. "You find us something low key enough that'll get us back to the airport, and then we can use my car," the retired Texas Ranger drawled. Then he grinned. "I can take this stupid hat off. That way the cops back there won't recognize me." He paused a moment, then added, "And don't you think it's about time you got rid of that silly-ass look of your own? Tell me, Cooper," he said, using the only name he'd ever known Bolan by, "Is it true blondes have more fun?"

Even considering the fact that they'd just lost their

first substantial lead toward Pepe 88, Bolan couldn't help but see the humor. It was impossible not to like the former blacksuit—the guy was one of the most genuine men the Executioner had ever met. Looking up into the rearview mirror, he removed the wig he'd put on right before the plane had touched down in Bogotá. The ash-blond mustache and beard came off next.

The Executioner now knew where the premonition that had precipitated his putting on the disguise at the last minute had come from. His instincts had warned him that Pepe 88 might have men at the airport who would see him arrive. As things had turned out, the disguise had served double-duty. It had not only hidden his face from the FARCs, it had done the same thing for the airport police.

"Now, *there's* the mysterious face I remember," Wilson said as Bolan finished pulling the last of the spirit gum adhesive from his face.

Closing the cab door behind him, Bolan stopped for a moment, patting himself down. He had the Beretta, Desert Eagle and a Tactical Operations SAW—Special Assault Weapon—knife. He also had his cell phone in his jacket pocket. Anything else he might need during the mission, he'd have to pick up as he went.

Bolan made his way along the row of parked cars. Spying a Toyota Highlander, he found the driver's door unlocked. A moment later, he had cracked the steering column with the butt of the Desert Eagle. Drawing the knife from the sheath at the small of his back, he jammed it into the hole and started the engine.

Wilson joined him, taking the passenger's seat. "You got us set up with a base house, I understand?" the Executioner asked.

"Oh yeah," the Texan replied. "One dilly of a base house."

Bolan nodded and backed out of the parking space. As he pulled out onto the street, he watched two Colombian National Police vehicles pull in behind the abandoned taxicab.

The big SUVs hadn't shielded the cab as long as he'd guessed they would.

But it had been long enough.

3

Wilson had driven from his home near Iquitos, Peru, and rented a small cottage on the edge of the jungle south of Bogotá. The sun had fallen and the moon risen high in the sky by the time he pulled his Ford Explorer off the rugged pathway that led from the highway to the house. Overhead, the Executioner could see the Southern Cross shining brightly in the sky.

Neither man spoke as they exited the vehicle and walked toward the steps leading to the house. Like many jungle dwellings, this cottage had been built on stilts to stave off flooding during the rainy season, which was what they were in, Bolan remembered, as a sudden shower began falling through the jungle leaves.

Wilson reached inside the pocket of his fatigue pants for the key as the two men ran up the steps. A moment later, they were inside the small house listening to the rain pound the tin roof like thousands of heavy hammers. Wilson struck a match and lit a kerosene lamp.

Bolan took a quick look around the single room. Two small sleeping lays were against opposite walls, with mosquito nets hanging over them. The only other furniture was a rough wooden table and two chairs.

But the room was far from empty. Wilson had

brought suitcases and duffle bags of all shapes, colors and sizes. Bolan had already seen the retired Ranger's fancy .45s. He wondered what other weapons the man might have hidden in his luggage.

"You have any trouble at the border?" Bolan asked as the two men dropped into the chairs on opposite sides of the table.

As Wilson shook his head, the kerosene lamp magnified his shadow into a giant, misshapen, cartoon-like umbra against the cheap plywood walls. "I used the same 'passport' I saw you using as I walked up toward the plane," he said. "Only I paid in Peruvian soles instead of pesos. The Colombian officials didn't seem to mind." He paused a moment, then chuckled so low it was barely audible above the continuing rain. "Remind me to have your director—or whoever it is who's in charge of that training center—reimburse me."

Bolan nodded in the eerie semidarkness. Wilson, like all soldiers and police officers selected for blacksuit training, had a very limited knowledge of Stony Man Farm. And knowing the real names of Bolan, Hal Brognola, or any of the other permanent personnel of the Farm wasn't included in that knowledge. But careful background investigations were conducted on blacksuit candidates, and psychological profiles were part of those checks. Among all of the other qualities necessary to make the cut, the men chosen had to understand, and not resent, the fact that they were on a need-to-know basis and there was a lot they didn't need to know.

"Let me rephrase that," the retired Ranger said. "Maybe *you* better ask him to reimburse me since I'd never find him—even if I tried."

Bolan shrugged. "I'll make sure you break even before we leave," he said.

A sudden increased downpour of rain was so loud on the tin roof that both men had to quit talking.

"Let's get down to business," Bolan finally said. "First, the attack at the airport means that the bad guys knew someone was coming in from out of the country to go after them. They even knew the time—at least the approximate time."

Wilson frowned. "Maybe," he said. "On the other hand, FARC has enough personnel to have kept a round-the-clock surveillance if they wanted to."

Bolan nodded. "Duly noted," he said. "So the bottom line is they know *something* is happening. But we don't know exactly what they know, or how much." He reached up and scratched the five-o'clock shadow that had started on his chin. He was glad that he'd taken the trouble of putting on the disguise before Grimaldi had landed. "At least they don't know what we look like."

Wilson stood up and quickly unzipped one of the bags scattered around the small room. Digging through its contents, he pulled out a manila envelope, then returned to the table and set it down. "The intel that came to me," he said, "which I found mysteriously on my coffee table, by the way, was that you were going after Pepe 88 and needed someone who knew the local ropes." He paused a moment, then laughed softly. "My house was locked tighter than a drum, and the security system was on. I still don't know how your man got in without tripping it." He pulled a file folder from the envelope, opened it and spread the contents across the table.

The Executioner looked down at the table to see at least a dozen intelligence reports as well as photos of

Pepe 88 and several of his men for whom warrants had been issued both in Colombia and the United States. "Do you know what the 88 in this guy's name means?" he asked Wilson.

"The number keeps changing," Wilson replied. "But it always goes *up* rather than down. It's supposed to be the number of men he's killed personally with his favorite weapon—a machete."

"Is that true or exaggerated?" Bolan asked.

Wilson shrugged. "Who knows?" he said. "These FARC assholes are no different than any other terrorist or criminal organization. Sometimes they let stories get blown all out of proportion for the psychological effect they produce. Scares the living hell out of the locals and the other organizations they deal with. On the other hand, it wouldn't surprise me if this number was accurate, either. Pepe real name is Carlos Gomez-Garcia, and he's one stone-cold killer."

Bolan sat back in the darkness and watched the shadowy wings of a moth—magnified several times by the light—flutter across the wall. "From what I've been told, Pepe lives the life of a cocaine king on his ranch in the jungle. Both the Colombian army, and the national police, have raided the place at least a dozen times. But he's never there. And neither are any of his henchmen. Just the servants."

The retired Ranger nodded. "They've even sent the *Junglas* in after him in Black Hawk helicopters," he said. "You familiar with them?"

Bolan watched his own giant shadow nod this time. "Highly trained commandos," he said. "The best of the best Colombia has to offer. A lot like our own Army Rangers or Special Forces."

Wilson's shadow nodded on the wall. "Some of our Special Forces are supposed to be down here as advisers, I've heard," he said. "But we—America, I mean—don't openly admit such things, of course. On the other hand, the DEA has had agents working with the Colombians for well over twenty years."

"If they're going in in Black Hawks, it means Pepe and his crew can't have more than about three minutes' warning from the noise," the Executioner said. "That's assuming he's got guards posted and listening, which I'm sure he does. That's not enough time for all of them to get away."

Wilson leaned forward and rested his forearms on the rough wooden table. "No, it isn't," he said in a quiet voice. "So I guess we both know what that means."

"Pepe has an inside man," Bolan said. "That was proved at the airport today. And whoever it is has to be high up the food chain. Which is why the Colombian president called *our Man*."

"And why the president called you," Wilson added, sitting back in his chair again. "Who all knows you're here?"

"Supposedly just me, you, the two presidents and the personnel at the Farm," Bolan said.

"You trust everybody at the Farm?"

"Implicitly," the Executioner said.

Wilson nodded again. That was good enough for him. "Thought so," he said. "So the leak has to be down here. And like you said, it has to be somebody high up—close to the Colombian president."

"Or at least somebody with access to him somehow," Bolan said.

"So," Wilson said. "What's the plan, Stan?"

"I'm not sure yet," Bolan said. The rain had let up.

Like most tropical downpours, this one had been heavy but short. Turning toward the bags scattered around the room, he said, "What did you bring with you?"

"Just my handguns and a couple of deep-cover hide-outs in case I needed them. Broke them all down into parts and scattered them around the luggage in case the dudes at the border decided to X-ray the bags. They didn't. Just passed me through." He paused a moment, then went on as if talking to himself. "I'd have never made it through any kind of thorough search. But a cursory exam is the norm—especially if you've paid up front like I did, and have either Colombian or Peruvian plates on your vehicle." He reached up, and ran his hand through his hair. "I was pretty much counting on *you* bringing the heavy artillery down with you."

"I did bring it with me," the Executioner said, thinking of the twin M-16s, the MP-5, and several other weapons he'd stashed on board before he and Grimaldi had left the United States. "But it flew away again when the plane had to take off."

Wilson shrugged. "Shit happens," he said. "I guess we just gotta work around it."

"We're not in too bad a shape for now with our pistols," Bolan said. "And we can pick up more guns and ammo as we go. I've got a feeling we're going to be putting quite a few gunmen down before this is all over. And it would be a shame to let perfectly good equipment go to waste."

Even in the low lighting, Bolan could see the retired Ranger smile. "Back in Texas," he said. "We wouldn't call that a shame. We'd call it a *sin*."

Bolan studied the man for a moment. Even though Wilson was less muscular than he remembered, the retired Texas Ranger was still a good sized man. "The rest of my luggage left Colombia with the armory," he finally said. "And I don't see a shopping mall anywhere around here in the trees. You suppose some of your clothes will fit me?"

"Might be a little tight, but you're welcome to take your pick," Wilson said. "All except one item."

"What's that?" the Executioner asked.

"My Ranger hat."

Bolan nodded. "Don't worry," he said. "It's all yours." He stood up. "Let's get our gear put together for tomorrow. And I need to clean my pistols, too. Then, if there's any time left, we'll drop inside those mosquito nets and grab a couple hours of sleep before we set out in the morning."

Wilson nodded his agreement. "Once the ball gets rolling downhill, there's not likely to be much time for rest." Standing up, he drew his matching .45s from under his khaki jacket, then set them on the table next to the lamp.

It was the first chance the Executioner had to look at them closely, and he saw that the twin 1911 Government Models could easily be on display at the Texas Ranger Museum in Waco. Each was heavily scroll-engraved, and both guns wore equally elaborately engraved scroll-design pewter grips.

"Guess I better give Becky and Betty a bath, too," Wilson said with a wide grin.

"Nice names," Bolan stated. "Can you can tell them apart?

"Oh, sure," Wilson drawled. "Betty's the surly one."

4

"Your knife have a name, too?" Bolan asked good-naturedly, thinking of Wilson's twin .45s—Becky and Betty—as the two men got dressed the next morning.

The Texan was inspecting what looked like the razor-sharp edge on a huge bowie knife he had pulled from one of his equipment bags. The blade was old and much-used, but well-maintained. It had a hardwood grip and a wide brass S-pattern guard. The blade looked to be around a foot long, about four inches at its widest but tapering to a needle-tipped clip point at the end. In the early-morning sunlight drifting in through the windows of the hut, the Executioner could see what was known as a swedge—or sharpened top edge—on the opposite side of the primary edge. He knew the swedge was used for that most devastating of all bowie-fighting techniques, the back cut. Along the spine of the knife, from guard to swedge, was a brass "blade catcher" strip. He figured the knife was an early to mid-1800s design.

"Oh, she's got a name, all right," Wilson said, grinning ear-to-ear. "I call her Bonnie."

Bolan shook his head as he pulled a borrowed black T-shirt over his head. It stretched tightly across the chest, but it would work. "Bonnie looks like she's got a few miles on her," he said.

"You better believe it," Wilson said. "This knife first belonged to my great-great grandfather," he said. "Family legend—and I don't know if this part's really true—is that old Grandpa was a friend of James Bowie's and had it forged similar to the one Jim was carrying at the time."

Bolan was pulling on a clean pair of Wilson's faded blue jeans. They were a little short. But like the T-shirt, they'd have to do in the present pinch. "I suppose now you're going to tell me your ancestor died with all the others at the Alamo," he said, a smile on his face to show Wilson he meant no disrespect.

The former Ranger laughed. He had already dressed in another pair of jeans, round-toed brown western boots, and a loose white cotton shirt. "No," he said. "But he fought at the Battle of San Jacinto, and was there when Santa Anna was captured. Later, when Sam Houston reorganized the Texas Rangers, he was one of the first on the roll sheet." Finally sheathing the big knife, he stuck it into his belt behind his back. "Becky and Betty" had already gone into his waistband on both hips.

Bolan slid his arms into the sound-suppressed Beretta's shoulder rig, checking to make sure it was secure and that the extra 9 mm magazines under his right arm were firmly in place. The big Desert Eagle returned to the belt-side holster on his strong side, with a double magazine pouch carrying extra .44 Magnums round clipped just in front of it. The small TOPS SAW knife was clipped behind his back in the same position where Wilson had put his bowie, and Bolan covered all three weapons and their accessories with the same short-sleeved safari-style jacket he had worn on the plane the day before. "You ready?" he asked.

"Almost," Wilson said. He unzipped a hard-sided hat box in the corner of the room. Pulling out a white straw Western hat he set it atop his head. Then, with a practiced hand, he adjusted it to a slight angle. Bolan noted the hatband. It was hand-crafted of smooth brown leather and featured small gold Texas Ranger conchos separated by white and brown braided waxed thread.

The Executioner nodded. The hatband would have been an undercover problem in Texas—maybe anywhere in the U.S. But official Texas Ranger hats had been available for years to anyone who had the cash. They could be ordered from the Ranger Museum in Waco, and, in Colombia, cowboy hats were as common as they were in America's Southwest. No one was going to give Wilson's hat a second look. And even if they did, he knew Wilson well enough to be sure the man would have some kind of story as to where the hat came from.

Bolan led the way down the steps to the Explorer and got in on the passenger's side. Wilson took the wheel, and a few minutes later they had bumped their way back across the jungle path to the highway and then on into Bogotá.

Colombia's capital city had a worldwide reputation as one of *the* most dangerous locations on the planet. It was midmorning when they reached the southern tip of the city.

Wilson had kept up a near nonstop monologue as they drove, filling Bolan in on the kind of on-the-ground local intelligence you couldn't get from tourist guides or even highly accurate reports. "There are exceptions," the man said. "But in a generalized way you can divide Bogotá into two parts. There's the north part of the city and the south. Neither part is Disneyland, but the south is the most dangerous. Up north you'll find the more affluent suburbs and such."

Bolan saw no need to reply. They would have to begin this operation at ground level and the most likely sources to give them a lead into Pepe 88 and the man's FARC 28th Front would be in the southern part of Bogotá. He directed Wilson to take him on a tour of the town in order to get a general feel for the place.

Pepe 88 and other narcoterrorists had left their marks on at least half of the hotels, travel agencies and most of the corporations that displayed American logos. In addition to the rubble they saw, Bolan could see that the streets were already lined with thieves, pickpockets, and low-level felons searching for any crime of opportunity.

Bolan directed his new partner into a parking space in front of an outdoor café. The men knew that eating, like sleeping, would become an unaffordable luxury once the game was afoot, so they took seats beneath an umbrella and ordered some food. The waiter brought out steaming plates filled with boiled meat, peas, carrots, and white and yellow potatoes covered in cream.

As they ate, Wilson repeated his question of the night before. "You come up with a plan of attack yet?"

Bolan swallowed a mouthful of beef, took a drink of unsweetened tea and said. "I've come up with a plan. Not a particularly good one. But the best available at the moment."

Wilson scraped his fork across his plate, scooping up several green peas. "Care to share it with me?"

Bolan twisted his head right and left to make sure there were no listening ears, then said, "The best I can come up with at the moment is that we start hitting the south side cantinas. Maybe we'll pick up on something. And we both might as well have 'gringo' stamped on our foreheads. That means we're ripe for kidnapping, which is as much a FARC specialty as blowing things up."

He knew kidnapping was a $350 million dollar a year industry in Colombia with close to two thousand people being abducted each year. Men like Pepe 88 were behind many such crimes. Becoming one of the victims might be the only chance he and Wilson would have into the organization.

"You do like to live dangerously, don't you?" the retired Ranger said as he stabbed his fork into a yellow piece of potato.

"I like doing whatever I have to do to get the job done," the Executioner replied.

Wilson smiled. "You'd have been a damn good Ranger," he said.

"Thanks," Bolan said. Lifting his wrist, he looked at his watch. "Let's get going."

He left money on the table and led Wilson back to the Explorer.

A half hour later the two men were seated at the bar of La Cantina Rosa, in the heart of a south side barrio. Bolan knew he had picked a good place when they walked through the door and all conversation stopped. The interior of the bar was almost as sparsely furnished as the cottage Wilson had rented, with rough-hewn tables and chairs, bar stools with ripped plastic seats, and a broken mirror above a long row of bottles. Both men ordered a beer and sat quietly as the talk behind them gradually returned to normal. The bartender gave them a quick look of amazement mixed with pity, then moved to the other end of the bar and struck up a conversation with an old man who'd had both hands amputated.

The Executioner watched out of the corner of his eye

as the elderly gentleman pushed the stubs at his wrist into the sides of his beer bottle, then lifted it carefully to his lips.

Fifteen minutes later, it was obvious the regulars were no longer paying any attention to the two visitors. Bolan dropped some coins on the bar top and stood up. "If anything was going to happen, it would have by now," he said under his breath. "Let's try some other place." He started for the door. "But be careful on the way out. That's as good a time for an abduction as any."

Wilson was right behind him. "Maybe I should hang a few fifty-thousand-peso bills out of my pockets," he said in an equally quiet voice.

The south side of Bogotá was hardly hurting for drinking establishments, and they left the Explorer where it was parked and walked down the cracked concrete sidewalk to another cantina. Conversation again ended abruptly as soon as their white skin appeared in the doorway. Moving toward the bar, the Executioner took in the room with a quick glance. Men wearing ragged straw hats, and shirts that would no longer even make good dust rags, sat scattered throughout at chairs and tables. Some stared at the two gringos. But many of the men's eyes had glazed over and were fixed in space.

"Remind me to have my wedding reception here if I ever get married," Wilson said under his breath.

Once more, the Executioner led the way to the bar. Ordering another beer for them both, he carefully watched the bartender's hands as the man uncapped the bottles and brought them forward.

Wilson was no Bogotá rookie, either. He knew the score almost as well as Bolan did and also watched the drinks carefully.

Local criminals were known to disable potential victims with scopolamine before robbing or kidnapping them. It was so easily obtained and prevalent within the outlaw community that Bogotá hospitals received an average of two thousand victims per month. Most commonly dispensed in liquid form, scopolamine rendered its victims unconscious almost immediately and often caused serious—and lasting—medical problems.

The bartender set the bottles on the bar and, satisfied that the beer inside had no unwanted additives, both Bolan and Wilson took sips.

But the atmosphere within the bar showed no more promise than that of the Rosa and a few minutes later they left. They tried a few more establishments in Bogotá's skid row and were greeted in all with similar disdain.

"Well?" Wilson finally said.

Bolan nodded, at the same time feeling himself frown. "Yeah," he said. "That was a total waste of time." They got back into the Explorer.

Wilson turned slightly behind the wheel to glance the Executioner's way. "You got a better idea?"

"I think so."

"Well, let's have it."

"I think we should go shopping," Bolan said.

5

Dressed in his new beige cotton suit, Bolan led the way back to the Explorer. Behind him, he could hear Wilson muttering under his breath. As he opened the door to the passenger's seat, the Executioner watched the retired Ranger walk around the hood of the vehicle to the driver's side. Wilson wore an equally expensive light weight suit. But he had opted for ice-cream white.

"Never, ever," Wilson said, shaking his head as he got behind the wheel. "No matter where I am, what I'm doing, or how important I think it is, am I going through *that* again."

Wilson drove away from the modern shopping center in the north part of Bogotá. In the rearview mirror, he saw the tailor's shop fade in the background.

"Don't worry about it, Paul," Bolan said with a poker face. "Señor Reynaldo just seemed to like you."

"Oh, he liked me all right," the Texan said as he twisted the steering wheel and guided the SUV onto the street. "He liked me a little too *much*, is all." He grimaced. "You see how damn long he took measuring my inseam?"

"For a minute there," Bolan said. "I thought we might have already found your date for tonight."

"Very funny," Wilson said. "Speaking of dates, you still haven't told me what this 'date' stuff is all about."

Before he could answer, Bolan spotted a bodega crammed between an office complex and a short strip mall on the busy four-lane street. "Pull in there, Paul," he directed Wilson.

Wilson did as ordered, and a few moments later the Executioner had gone up to the small stand and returned with a gallon jug of a local red wine and a fifth of gin.

"Okay, we've both got new suits, we're going on a double date, and now I guess we're planning to get our dates drunk so we can get laid, right?" Wilson asked, his Texas drawl reflecting sarcasm.

"Not exactly," Bolan said as he strapped himself back into his seat.

Wilson couldn't keep a straight face any longer. "There's a pharmacy on every corner selling roofies down here if that's what you want." He laughed.

"You're misreading things," Bolan said. "Give me a chance and I'll explain it all to you while we drive. In the meantime, do you know where there's a high-end car rental place around here?"

Wilson nodded. "I should have guessed we'd need something classier than this old pile of nuts and bolts for the date," he said in mock anger. "My feelings are hurt."

"We've been fishing for leads so far," Bolan said. "But we've been fishing in the wrong lakes. And with the wrong bait.'

"Okay," Wilson said. "Go on."

"We need to go somewhere where we're more likely to find a FARC connection than these dives we've been hitting. Plus, like I said, we haven't been using the right bait." He paused, looking out the window as they continued north, deeper into the more affluent areas of the Colombian capital.

"I'm still listening," Wilson replied.

"We've seen nothing but drunken old men and petty thieves so far," the Executioner said. "One of the reasons is that we've hit the wrong places. The other is that we don't look like easy enough marks." He cleared his throat, then went on. "We're gringos all right. But we aren't the right kind of gringos."

"Not sure I'm following you," Wilson said with a frown.

"Then look in the mirror," Bolan said. "In addition to both being pretty good-sized fit guys, we've got the scars and hardness in our faces that say we've seen the bad side of things and lived to tell about it."

The retired Texas Ranger caught on all at once. "And there's always an easier-looking mark close by," he said.

"Exactly," Bolan said. "So what we have to do is counterbalance that hardness in other ways. The suits are just the beginning. They spell money—money that's worth taking us on.'

"And the wine and gin?" Wilson asked.

"Another part of the illusion. We'll wash our mouths out and splash a little on like aftershave and anyone within smelling distance will think we rich guys have been on a bender."

Ahead, Bolan saw the car rental lot. Wilson pulled the Explorer into the parking lot.

Ten minutes later, the Executioner drove away in a shiny BMW, followed Wilson to an upscale shopping mall, then left the car running while the Texan parked the Explorer, locked it up and walked back to him carrying a small soft-sided grip.

The two men had removed all of their weapons before going to the tailor for their fittings, and had stashed them in the bag.

When Wilson had taken the passenger's seat, Bolan said, "We may have to lock those up in the trunk. If we're lucky, and FARC does kidnap us, a .44 Magnum and a sound-suppressed 9 mm aren't going to help our covers. Not to mention Betty, Becky and Bonnie."

"You're right of course," Wilson said. "And you know…I think that's the first time in my life that I've ever heard anyone suggest getting kidnapped would be *lucky*." Without waiting for a response from Bolan, he unzipped the bag. "I don't know about you," he went on, "but I've got a definite aversion to going into something like this completely unarmed. So I brought along a couple of my favorite toys." Reaching into the bag, he pulled out two small gun rugs. As Bolan drove slowly out of the parking lot, Wilson unzipped the first and held up a North American Arms Black Widow minirevolver. It was less than six inches in overall length and not quite four inches tall.

"Five rounds of .22 Magnum hollowpoints," the retired Ranger said with a grin. "Or, as I prefer to think of it, two and a half .44 Mags like that big *Star Wars* lookin' thing of yours."

The Executioner started south on the same thoroughfare through the city that had brought them north. "What's in the other case?" he asked.

Wilson unzipped the other rug and pulled out another tiny North American Arms pistol. But this one was a semiautomatic. "Guardian .380," the Texan said. "You can hide it in places most kidnappers aren't going to check. Especially on a couple of rich, drunken gringos."

"Which one's mine?" the Executioner asked.

"Well, you're running the show, Cooper, so it's your call."

Bolan shook his head as he began weaving in and out of the late-afternoon traffic. "They're your guns," he said. "I can live with either one."

"Then I'll keep the Black Widow," Wilson said, handing the .380 to the Executioner. "Always had a soft spot for the old single-actions. Must be the Ranger in me."

Bolan took the tiny pistol and dropped it in the side pocket of his new jacket for the time being. "Open the gin bottle," he said.

Wilson shook his head in mock disbelief. "Drinking and driving?" he asked as he twisted the cap. "All my illusions about you guys at the Farm—truth, justice, the American way—all shot to hell now." But Bolan had already told him what the alcohol was for, and Wilson took a swig, rolled it around in his mouth, gargled a few times, then spit it out on the floor of the BMW. "That should add to the olfactory ambience inside the car, here," he said. He passed the bottle to Bolan.

The Executioner drove with his elbows for a moment while he poured an ounce or so of gin into the palm of his hand, then rubbed it into his face and neck. The alcohol bit into his skin, burning slightly. He took his own mouthful before returning the bottle to Wilson. A moment later, he spit it out on the floor between his feet.

The sun was falling behind the taller buildings of Bogotá, and dusk had engulfed the city. "So now maybe you better explain what you meant about these *dates* you keep mentioning," Wilson said.

"We also need a couple of guides," Bolan said. "Does Bogotá have a red light district?"

"What?"

"A red light district," Bolan repeated. "You know. An area where—"

"I *know* what a red light district is," Wilson said, blowing air out between his lips in confusion again. "This whole city is one *gigantic* red light district."

"Then you think you could direct me somewhere where we could find a couple of say…medium-priced hookers?"

"I expect I could do that," the retired Ranger said with a deadpan expression on his face. "Not that I've ever partaken of such services myself. But I have heard the older boys talking in the locker room." He shook his head, showing the Executioner that he was still confused about this whole new plan of attack. But Bolan could tell the retired Ranger had also decided to trust his judgment.

That didn't mean, however, that Wilson didn't still have questions. "Why do you want *medium-priced* hookers?" he asked the Executioner.

"Because a couple of well-dressed men about town such as ourselves wouldn't look right with street girls," Bolan said. "And the top-of-the-line call girls probably wouldn't have the connections we need."

The BMW came to a stoplight and Wilson squinted through the diminishing sunlight at the sign announcing the cross street. "When the light changes," he said, "make a left."

6

They found the girls working the downtown area just off the Plaza de Bolivar. Dressed in short tight skirts and thin halter tops, they stood awaiting their first customers of the evening in front of a mural on the side of a white brick building. The painting commemorated Colombia's abolition of slavery in 1851.

The contradiction before his eyes wasn't lost on the Executioner. Formal slavery had been banned well over 150 years before, but many Colombian nationals—these women included—had fallen victim to other forms of servitude.

The women moved up to the driver's window, and Bolan could see that the taller one had bleached blond hair that contrasted dramatically with her olive skin. The shorter of the two wore her brunette locks long and braided. Both of the women were attractive, and both would fit the bill for what Bolan wanted. The only coaxing it took to get them into the car was the flashing of a few bills.

Bolan threw the BMW back into Drive as soon as the blonde—who identified herself as Dolores—had taken the passenger's seat as Wilson got into the back with the braided Josefa.

They had barely pulled away from the curb when Josefa lifted the gallon jug of wine from the floor of the back seat, unscrewed the cap and lifted it to her lips. She gurgled down several swallows before handing it over the seat to Dolores, who did the same. When she then tried to hand the wine to the Executioner, he declined. Slurring his words slightly, he said, "That's for you girls. My buddy and I are sticking to the gin."

That seemed fine with the two prostitutes.

Bolan had studied Wilson's Stony Man Farm training file on the flight down with Grimaldi, and remembered that the man had been regarded as one of the Texas Rangers' best undercover operatives.

"Damn, you gals are purty," Wilson said as they drove away from the plaza. He used his fist to raise his hat higher on his forehead for a better look. "Good thing we're rich, 'cause I can tell you don't come cheap."

The two prostitutes giggled like schoolgirls at the compliment.

"Fact is," Wilson went on, "you're so fine I hate to bring up business. But how much is this gonna cost my buddy and me?"

"That depends on what you want," Josefa said, snuggling up next to him. "And how many times you want it.'

Dolores laughed. She moved closer to Bolan and began rubbing his leg.

"Well, girls," Wilson said, "I tell you what. We don't know exactly what we want yet, but I know we're gonna want it for the whole night. How about we all go out, do a little more drinkin' and some dancin', then we can all head back to the hotel room and make us one big pile on the bed?"

"That will cost more, of course," Dolores said, speaking to Bolan in the front seat. "For the whole night."

Wilson had heard the blonde and answered for Bolan. "Well, hell, sweet thing," he said, leaning forward. "What's money for if not spendin'?"

They continued to cruise down the street as the women downed more wine. "You ladies know a good place to go kick up your boot heels?" Wilson asked.

"Your hotel is fine, like you said," Josefa told him. "But we are not wearing boots if that's what you wanted."

Wilson cut loose with a laugh. "That wasn't the kind of 'boot kickin' I meant, darlin'," he said when he'd regained control of himself. "Kickin' up your boot heels is another way of sayin' dancin' where I come from."

"And where do you come from?" Josefa asked, stroking Wilson's hair.

"Why, Texas, of course!" the former Ranger said.

"You are here on business?" Dolores quietly whispered into Bolan's ear.

Bolan nodded. "Oil," he said. "We're buying up drilling rights."

Wilson, still playing his part as the loud, drunken Texan, overheard the words and said, "Hey, you girls know what Texas and Colombia have in common?" When neither of them answered, he bellowed out, "Oil, and damn fine lookin' women!"

In the rearview mirror, Bolan saw Josefa point down toward the gin bottle Wilson held gripped between his knees. "Do you need anything else?" she asked.

"Just a place to put it, baby," the retired Ranger said.

This brought the women to hysterical laughter. "I was pointing at the *bottle*," Josefa said. "I meant, would you like anything besides alcohol? We know where to get cocaine if you'd like some."

"Well, hell, I reckon you would know!" Wilson said. "This bein' Bogotá after all. Maybe later. Always wanted to try a little of that stuff." He paused, and for a moment, the car went silent, and Bolan continued to drive. "Hey, you know what I *would* like to do?" he said. "Go meet one of them 'cocaine king' guys. I'd buy some of that stuff off him just to meet him. You know, one of them guys like Al Pacino in *Scarface*."

Dolores and Josefa were left with blank looks on their faces.

"Better even than that," Wilson said, almost shouting in false drunkenness. "I'd like to meet one of them...whadaya call 'em? You know, them terrorists? What are they called...farts?"

The two prostitutes laughed uproariously. "FARCs," Dolores said, tears of true mirth streaming down her face next to Bolan. "Not farts!"

"Well, whatever you call 'em," Wilson said. "Think we could meet one of them? They sell cocaine too, don't they?"

Bolan watched out of the corner of his eye as Dolores and Josefa exchanged quick conspiratorial glances. Then Josefa said, "Sure, honey. The FARCs sell it, too. And I think we could arrange a meeting for you—you two being such important American businessmen." Another quick glance passed between the two women.

"If you will find a pay phone," Dolores told Bolan, "I will call and see if it can be arranged."

"Why, hell, darlin'," Wilson said. "This is the space age." He reached inside the pocket of his new suit coat. "Use my cell phone."

After another quick look at Dolores, Josefa said, "Oh, no. No cell phones! They will never answer or talk business over a cell phone. It is too easy to be overheard."

"Damn," Wilson said, pulling his empty hand back out of his coat. "I shoulda knowed that." He leaned toward the front seat. "Find the lady a phone booth, will ya, pardner?"

In the rearview mirror, the Executioner could see the retired Ranger undercover expert's face, and he looked like an excited ten-year-old boy. "Dammit!" Wilson said. "This is gonna be one hell of a night, old buddy. We're gonna meet us a real live fart…I mean FARC cocaine king just like the newspapers is always talkin' about! And then we're gonna drill these two honeys like a couple of thousand-foot oil wells!"

Bolan had been happy to step back and let the other man carry the ball on this leg of the mission, playing "straight man" to Wilson's "rich and stupid Texas oilman" character. And he was impressed. He had seen few men, outside of Stony Man's Leo Turrin, who could step into a role and play it as well as this former blacksuit.

Ahead, Bolan saw a gas station. A pay phone had been bolted to the side of the building and he pulled up next to it. Both women started to get out.

Wilson reached out drunkenly for Josefa but missed. "Hey, sweet thing!" he said. "Come on back here! It don't take botha you on the phone, and you an' me could sit here and wait an' do us a little snoggin', don't you think?"

Josefa frowned for a moment, then closed the door behind her and accompanied Dolores to the phone on the wall.

As soon as they were alone again, Wilson broke character and leaned forward in his seat. "Looks like it's going to work," he told Bolan. "Unless I miss my guess, we're being set up for a snatch."

Bolan's eyes were glued on the women against the gas station wall. Dolores had dialed a number and was speaking into the receiver. But every few seconds she glanced nervously toward the BMW. Josefa, standing next to her, did the same.

"I think you're right," the Executioner said. "Notice how they haven't hit us up for a specific amount of money for their night's services?"

"Yeah," Wilson said. "That struck me as a little funny, too."

"They stopped talking about money about the time you mentioned wanting to meet a FARC," Bolan said. "That's because now they see an opportunity for a much bigger score than they'd get for a night of sex." He paused, smiling at Dolores as she looked anxiously through the windshield at him. Then, turning sideways on the off chance that the women could read lips, he said, "They'll be getting a nice finder's fee for us."

"Makes sense," the retired Ranger said.

"You're putting on one heck of a performance, by the way," Bolan said.

"Coming from you, that's one terrific compliment," Wilson replied. "In my time I've played everything from outlaw biker to environmental terrorist. Acting always came pretty easy to me." He let another chuckle escape his chest. "On the other hand, you know what everybody in the other forty-nine states always says."

"What's that?" the Executioner asked.

"Nobody can be as loud or obnoxious, or lie like a Texan."

Bolan nodded back at the man. Paul Wilson was turning out to be an excellent asset on this mission. Through the glass, he watched Dolores continue to speak into the receiver of the ancient black rotary telephone. Occasionally, she paused to consult Josefa, then returned to the conversation she was carrying on with whoever it was on the other end of the line. Finally, she glanced one last time toward Bolan, spoke a few more words into the phone, then hung up. She and Josefa returned to the car.

"It is all arranged," Dolores said as the two women got back into the BMW. There was a tinge of anxiety in her words—an anxiety that two men as drunk as Bolan and Wilson apparently were would be likely to ignore. "You will get to meet your FARC," she said. "And you will get to buy some cocaine from him if you like."

"Hot damn!" Wilson shouted. "This is gonna be more fun than when the pigs ate my little brother!"

Dolores and Josefa looked at each other, slightly confused. Then Dolores looked into the back seat and said in a low voice, "You must be very careful how you treat this man. Remember, he is a terrorist. He is only meeting you as a favor to me."

Bolan knew the warning was just part of the show. The women had picked up on the fact that Wilson wanted to see how close to the fire he could get without being burned.

"Hell, sweetheart," the retired Ranger said. "Danger is my middle name!"

Dolores smiled thinly at Josefa in the back seat, then turned her attention back to Bolan. "We are meeting this man at the Disco Asesinato," said the bleached blonde.

Bolan nodded. Considering what he knew they

were about to get themselves into, the name seemed appropriate.

Asesinato was Spanish for "murder."

7

As in any big city the world over, Bogotá had no definite line of demarcation dividing the right and wrong sides of the tracks. But as he pulled the rented BMW into the parking lot of the *Disco Asesinato*, the Executioner could tell they were somewhere in the no-man's land in between.

"Hot damn!" Wilson shouted from the back seat. "I'm ready to dance! Disco down and dirty, girls!"

Dolores and Josefa exchanged nervous smiles.

Bolan had watched the women closely since the phone call. They were prostitutes, pure and simple, and setting their tricks up for a FARC kidnapping appeared to be something fairly new to them. What they were doing was wrong—one hundred percent wrong. But the Executioner, nevertheless, hoped there would be a way out of this situation where they didn't get hurt. He had known, and worked with, many such women during his career—they made some of the best informants money, or anything else, could buy.

He knew there was always some determining factor that had led them to selling their bodies—and with those bodies, their souls.

The Executioner pulled the BMW into an empty

parking space against the side of the building and got out. Playing the part of ladies now, Dolores and Josefa waited for him and Wilson to open their doors for them.

Bolan scanned the parking lot as they approached the front door. There was a mixture of every kind of vehicle imaginable on the gravel outside the disco—everything from other BMWs, Cadillacs and Corvettes to broken-down pickup trucks.

And he knew, somewhere in the mix was the vehicle he and Wilson would be shoved into after their kidnapping.

Bolan opened the glass front door and Dolores and Josefa walked through. "Remember the scopolamine," the Executioner whispered to Wilson as the man brought up the rear of the party.

The retired Texas Ranger nodded his head.

The music—loud enough that Bolan had been able to hear it in the parking lot—blasted out of the main room into the entryway as the Executioner stepped inside the club and let the door swing shut behind him. A man wearing a white suit and open-collared bloodred shirt approached, a smile on his face. He seemed to recognize the two women, nodded, then glanced up at Bolan and Wilson. "Follow me, please," he said in heavily accented English, then turned and led them into the main room.

Bolan dropped back to replace Wilson, bringing up the rear of the group. Brightly colored strobe lights flashed across the dance floor as the man in the white suit led them to a table in the middle of the room. Huge brown clay planters, the vines and leaves of every type of tropical greenery imaginable growing out of them, were spaced between the tables, giving the room a unique jungle atmosphere. The Executioner was pleased as he pulled Dolores's chair out to seat her. The planters, he suspected, would come in handy in the next few minutes.

The man in the white suit disappeared and a waitress wearing a short black leather skirt suddenly stood at their table, taking orders for drinks. Bolan ordered a shot of tequila, as did Wilson. Both women wanted rum and Coke.

Conversation was nearly impossible over the loud music that blared from the disc jockey's booth set high in the wall across the room from where they sat. Dolores moved her chair closer to Bolan's as they waited for their drinks, She reached under the table to stroke his thigh. "You like that, no?" she shouted into his ear.

Bolan just smiled and nodded.

A few minutes later, the waitress returned with their drinks. Bolan and Wilson exchanged quick glances of understanding.

Neither man planned to drink. They knew both shot glasses had probably been laced with something that would knock them out.

Bolan stared at the small glass as one of the strobe lights passed over them. The liquid in the glass was slightly cloudier than it should have been. That meant the bartender had added the drug in powdered form.

When the waitress left, Bolan shouted over the music. "I've changed my mind," he told Dolores. "That rum and Coke looks better to me." Without waiting for a reply, he moved the shot glass in front of her and pulled the larger drink across the table.

For a second, a horrified look passed over Dolores's face. But then she covered it well, saying, "But I *hate* tequila!"

Bolan pulled a large peso note from his pocket. "That

ought to cover your discomfort," he said, dropping the note next to the shot glass.

The woman thought well on her feet. "It helps," she said, as the money quickly disappeared down her low neckline into her bra. "But not enough." Waving a hand at their waitress, who was passing by with another tray of drinks, she ordered the woman to take the tequila away and bring another rum and Coke.

Bolan had been watching Wilson out of the corner of his eye and was reminded that Dolores was not the only one who could think on her feet. With the women's attention turned toward the waitress, the Texan had leaned backward in his chair and dumped his tequila into one of the planters behind him.

By the time the waitress had left again and the women turned back to the table, Wilson was smacking his lips and shouting out, "*Viva* tequila! It's the only decent drink for a son of the Alamo!"

Like so many other things Wilson had been saying that evening, the Alamo reference was lost on Dolores and Josefa. But they chalked it up to just another mindless outburst from a typically drunk and stupid American. They both frowned, however, when the retired Ranger was still conscious a few minutes later.

Dolores leaned over to her friend. With the music screaming the only word Bolan caught was *erroneo,* Spanish for mistake.

He watched Josefa glance quickly to her drink. She made no move to touch it. The women were clearly confused, and afraid to touch their own drinks, worrying that the bartender had accidentally poured the drug meant for Wilson's tequila into one of their drinks.

Wilson, still playing the part of loud and obnoxious

drunk, leaned over the table and yelled out, "Where's this FARC guy we're supposed to meet?"

Both women recoiled in horror, shushing him, with Josefa reaching out to place a hand over his mouth. "Keep your voice down!" she warned. "This man is dangerous. Do you want *everyone* to hear?"

"Aw, hell honey," Wilson shouted out when Josefa removed her hand. "It's louder than a West Texas tornado in here. Ain't nobody paying us no attention anyway!"

That was hardly the case. Bolan could see that the word FARC had caused the heads of everyone at the tables within their immediate vicinity to turn toward Wilson. But a few seconds later, everyone had turned away again.

The waitress returned and more drinks were ordered. Dolores leaned up to whisper in the woman's ear this time. Bolan heard none of her words. But he saw the waitress nod conspiratorially before she left.

"We should dance!" Josefa said loudly, turning to Wilson. She still had a puzzled look on her face, surprised the man was conscious. Bolan suspected she wanted the retired Ranger to exert himself and shoot the knockout drug through his system.

Bolan knew Wilson would not get by with dumping yet another drink into the planter. And he couldn't exchange his own glass with Dolores's again, either.

Leaning in to Dolores, Bolan said, "My buddy's been drinking all day and he's a little obnoxious. Sorry."

Dolores played her part well. "No, no!" she shouted over the music. "He is just having a good time!"

"On the other hand," the Executioner said, "we *would* like to hook up with the guy we came here to meet."

"I am sure he is on his way," Dolores said.

No sooner had the words left her mouth than Bolan saw a young man wearing tight blue jeans, a gold Western belt buckle, cowboy boots, and a tan leather blazer appear in the doorway. The young man looked to be no more than twenty years old as he stood on the edge of the room, scoping out the disco. Finally, his eyes fell on Bolan and Wilson, and he smiled as he made his way toward them.

Bolan frowned, recognizing the young man for what he was, a *sicario*—one of Colombia's teenaged professional assassins. Stony Man Farm intelligence had reported that there were as many as three thousand of these youthful freelance hit men. Typically, they were contracted by drug dealers, businessmen and sometimes even the Colombian police to get rid of competition. But Bolan had never heard of the FARCs using these youthful murderers.

The FARCs had enough stone-cold killers of their own. They didn't have to farm out their wet work to *anyone*.

Something was wrong.

Bolan watched the young man approach their table. Dolores and Josefa looked up and saw him, then both women leaned inward. "He is here!" Josefa shouted over the blasting music.

The Executioner saw Wilson frown at the man. "He looks a little young to me," the former Ranger said.

"Do not let his youth fool you!" Dolores yelled. "He is…what you wanted to meet." Turning to the young man, she added, "Felipe! Pull up a chair!"

The young man did just that, grabbing a chair from the next table without bothering ask the occupants if they needed it. The couple at the table, in their midthirties, turned away quickly. They had recognized the killer for what he was.

A moment later, Felipe was seated between Dolores and Josefa. He frowned slightly at both Bolan and Wilson, then glanced at their drinks. Obviously, he had expected the men to be unconscious upon his arrival.

Introductions were made by the women, and Bolan and Wilson shook the young man's hand. But before anyone could say more, the waitress returned with new drinks. After placing them on the table, she looked at Felipe.

The young man shook his head and the woman walked away quickly, the expression on her face telling Bolan she was relieved not to have to deal with him further.

Just then a shoving match broke out on the dance floor with two men facing off. The problem seemed to be an attractive young Colombian woman. The problem somehow resolved itself and the dancing resumed.

When he looked back to the table, the Executioner saw that Wilson's glass was empty.

Wilson had gone stiff, sitting straight up in his chair. All of the other people at the table stared at the retired Ranger as he slurred out, "Funny…I feel…funny…like something is…." As the last word left his mouth he fell forward onto the table, his forehead hitting it with a bang that could even be heard over the music.

Bolan had yet to touch his own, undoubtedly doctored, drink. He shook his head in mock disgust, then turned to Dolores. "I'm surprised this didn't happen earlier," he said. "Like I told you, he's been drinking since we got up this morning."

Felipe seemed more than prepared to take charge. "We should get him out to your car," the young man said. "There are thieves and killers all over Bogotá who would take advantage of him in this condition." The young man couldn't quite keep the ironic smile off his lips as the words passed them.

Bolan nodded, stood up and started toward Wilson.

"You can finish your drink first, if you like," Felipe said, looking down at the glass in front of the Executioner.

Bolan shook his head. "No, I've had enough. And somebody's got to babysit this drunk on the way back to the hotel. I'll just pay the tab and we'll get out of here."

The young assassin clearly wasn't pleased. Bolan was twice his size and conscious. Just the same, he played along, helping the Executioner lift Wilson out of his chair and drag him toward the door. Bolan knew he was undoubtedly armed, and probably had friends waiting in the parking lot.

The women followed, chattering under their breath as Bolan and Felipe carried Wilson through the main room to the entryway. A few of the disco's more naive patrons snickered as they passed, thinking Wilson had simply consumed so much alcohol that he'd passed out. Other more savvy men and women took a quick look at Wilson, then Felipe, and an expression of pity fell over their faces.

The greeter in the white suit was nowhere to be seen as Bolan and Felipe carried Wilson into the parking lot. Felipe stopped outside the front door, staring straight ahead without speaking.

"Our car's this way," Bolan said, tugging Wilson. "Come on."

Felipe didn't budge.

Before Bolan could say more, a white van came roaring into the parking lot, then skidded across the gravel to a halt right in front of them. The side door contained a darkly tinted window. It slid open suddenly and two men wearing green fatigues jumped out, aiming AK-47s at Bolan and Wilson. Black stocking caps covered their heads and faces.

"Get in!" screamed the taller of the two.

"Hey, what——" Bolan said, feigning surprise.

The tall man stepped out and brought the butt of his Russian assault rifle around, catching Bolan on the chin.

The Executioner stumbled backwards. Then, catching his balance, he helped Felipe carry Wilson to the open door of the van as he was prodded in the ribs with the barrel of one of the AK-47s. More green-clad arms reached out, pulling the retired Ranger on board.

Bolan continued to act groggy as he was pushed and pulled into the van. The seats had been removed from the rear of the vehicle, and he was thrown to the floor next to where Wilson already lay, eyes still closed. Bolan continued to act dazed as he watched first Felipe, then Dolores and Josefa, reach out and accept short stacks of peso notes from one of the men.

Just before the door slid closed behind them, Bolan glanced toward Wilson. The retired Texas Ranger opened one eye, winked at him, then closed it again.

The man behind the wheel threw the van in gear, and they skidded out of the parking lot. Bolan opened his eyes but let a glazed look fall over them, as if he were still only half-conscious from the rifle blow. He noted that two of the AK-47s were still trained his way. The other two were on Wilson.

The tall man who had hit him with the rifle stock stepped forward now. Quickly, he ran his hands up and down Wilson's legs, then around his waist and over his chest and back. He did the same with Bolan, checking for weapons but not expecting to find any on these idiotic, drunken, yet wealthy Americans.

Stepping back, the tall man pulled the stocking cap from his head and dropped it on the floor of the van. "Congratulations," he said. "You are now in the hands of *Autodefensas Unidas de Colombia*, and you will be well taken care of. At least until your companies pay the six-million-dollar ransom we shall be requiring of them."

Bolan didn't react to the news. They had been kidnapped by the wrong men.

Autodefensas Unidas de Colombia, or AUC as they were more commonly called—was a right-wing paramilitary organization which, like FARC, financed their operations through drug dealing and kidnapping for ransom. But considering the fact that they were at opposite ends of the political poll from their left-wing counterparts, they were the natural enemies of FARC. And were not likely to have any connections to Pepe 88.

The fatigue-clad gunmen had all exposed their faces. Bolan was well aware that could mean only one thing. They had no intentions of letting Bolan and Wilson go free whether they were paid six million dollars or not.

Bolan gradually allowed himself to come around from the rifle blow. But he took his time, evaluating the situation around him as he pretended to return to his senses.

Three men in fatigues—all with AK-47s in their hands and pistols on their belts—were in the back of the van. Two still aimed their rifles toward Bolan and Wilson. The third—the tall man who had spoken—was leaning over the front seat and conversing with the driver. A fifth man sat in the shotgun seat.

The Executioner faced a dilemma. He needed more information in order to put together an escape plan. But the only way he could get that information was to ask questions. The men holding them hostage might refuse to answer. What they would certainly do, however, was realize he was fully cognizant.

So far, Bolan had seen no handcuffs or other restraints. But that didn't mean there weren't any on board the van. Wilson had been left untethered because they thought he was unconscious. And they hadn't been too anxious to tie up the Executioner because he'd been stunned by the rifle blow and had more rifles pointing at his head and chest. But if they suddenly realized he'd recovered from the strike to the chin he might be trussed up immediately.

As was his rule, the Executioner went with his instincts. He had to know more about their current situation if he were to get Wilson and himself out of it. And staying silent wasn't the way to glean that intelligence. He would have to gamble, taking his chances on being restrained.

"Where…where are we going?" Bolan asked in the meekest Spanish he could muster.

The tall man who had hit him with the rifle stock turned around. "For a little ride," he said. "You don't need to know more."

"I do if you want my company to pay the ransom," Bolan said, still faking sheepishness. "Not that they're going to cough up six million for the two of us." He paused and made a point of swallowing hard. "We're just not worth that much."

The tall man grinned. "There is some room for negotiation," he told the Executioner. "It's like any business."

Bolan shook his head. "There'd better be a lot of room or my friend and I are done for," he almost whispered. He had said the words on purpose. They were a tacit disavowment of any plans to fight back. And that meekness would sink into the AUC men's minds, either consciously or unconsciously.

The van continued through town, then out of the city. From where he sat on the floor, the Executioner's view through the tinted window was limited. About all he knew for certain was that they were headed north.

The problem he had anticipated came at a time he had not expected—after several minutes of silence had gone on while the van drove farther out of Bogotá. The tall man, who had gone back to conversing with the driver, suddenly turned around and shouted out, "Jorge. Cuff him." As soon as the words had left his mouth he twisted toward the front seat again.

A thick-chested man with a full beard moved from his sitting position to his knees and crabbed his way to Bolan's side. Pulling a set of handcuffs from the front pocket of his green fatigue pants, he reached out, grabbed Bolan's right arm and clamped the ratchets around his wrist. "Turn around," he ordered in a gruff voice.

The Executioner continued to sound as humbled as possible. "I can't," he said. "It'll kill the arthritis in my shoulders. Can't you just do it in front?" He glanced around the van. Then, knowing it would strike at the very heart of the bearded man's Colombian machismo, he said, "Surely six of you with big guns like you've got aren't afraid to handcuff one man in front."

The tall man heard the request and turned around again. Jorge looked to him for his orders. The leader of the pack looked down at the Executioner with pure contempt, then finally nodded to his minion. "Cuff him in front," he said. "But run them through his belt. And put the belt buckle behind him."

Jorge nodded, reached out and unbuckled the Executioner's belt before yanking it free of the loops. Then, only running it back through the two loops nearest the front, he buckled it behind Bolan's back as he'd been ordered. The handcuff dangling from the big American's right hand went beneath the leather, then up and onto his left wrist, essentially turning his own belt into a belly chain.

As Jorge moved toward Wilson—who had fallen to his side and lay snoring on the floor—the tall man turned around yet again and said, "Forget it. He'll be out for hours."

Bolan tested his reach with the handcuffs in front of him. He found that he could move them roughly six inches, up or down. And he figured he could probably get another inch or so of reach by snapping down and ripping the belt loops from his pants.

It wasn't much. But when the time came, he hoped it would be enough. If it wasn't, he and Wilson were as good as dead.

Jorge resumed his seat across from Bolan. Onward they drove into the night with the van growing darker as they drew farther away from the lights of the city. Twenty minutes or so after they'd been captured, the tall man talking to the driver turned around for good and sat down, his rifle across his lap, the hole in the barrel pointed at Bolan's abdomen. "Who do you work for?" he demanded.

"Gulf Oil," Bolan said quietly. "We're trying to work out a partial merger with Occidental Petroleum down here." He paused, raised his hand toward his mouth to cough, but stopped it far below the height to which it could have risen and coughed anyway before saying, "Excuse me." The little pantomime was yet another subtle message to the green-clad men with the Soviet rifles. And that message was that his range of motion was far more limited than it actually was.

The biggest problem he had, Bolan knew, was that there was no way to communicate with Wilson. He had decided that the best time to strike against their abductors would be the moment the van began to slow down before stopping at wherever it was they were going. It would be dangerous because the vehicle would still be moving, meaning they might wreck. Even if they didn't wreck, the driver could swerve at any unforseen moment and throw what Bolan had planned off course.

On the other hand, the same swerving could throw the rounds of the AK-47s off target just as well. But the biggest advantage was that the AUC men would be least expecting resistance at that moment.

Of course if he couldn't learn their destination ahead of time such problems were moot anyway—Bolan wouldn't know if they were stopping for good or stopping because they'd come to a stop sign he couldn't see. He felt himself begin to frown in concentration but willed the expression away. He wanted fear on his face at all times. He had to do everything in his power to convince the AUC terrorists that he was a mild-mannered oil executive who had no plans of resisting in any way. But that didn't mean he couldn't talk.

"Sir," he said quietly to the tall man.

"What?"

"What…er, what should I call you?"

"Gonzales," the tall man said. "You may call me Gonzales."

"Mr. Gonzales," the Executioner said meekly, "can't you…I mean could you…could you at least tell me where you're going to keep us? I've got claustrophobia and I'm scared to death of—"

Gonzales clenched his teeth tightly in scorn. "I suppose it cannot hurt anything," he said. "We'll be underground. But it won't be in a confined—"

"Underground!" Bolan almost shouted out. "No, no way, no I can't—"

Gonzales reached over and backhanded Bolan across the face. "Shut up and *listen*, you sniveling fool," he said, his teeth still clenched. "It won't be in a small confined space like you fear. We're approaching Zipaquira where the salt mines are located. There's an abandoned mine we can drive right into. Then its just a short walk into a cavern the size of a cathedral." He paused for a moment, then added, "Does that put your frightened little mind to rest?"

"I...guess so," Bolan said. "At least a little.'

Gonzales turned his head away. It was obvious he could no longer stand the sight of the Executioner—yet another aspect of their abduction Bolan knew he might be able to capitalize upon.

Ten minutes later, the driver spoke over his shoulder. "We are almost there, Gonzales," he said.

Wilson, who had continued snoring away throughout the ride, chose that moment to roll onto his back and shove his right hand down the front of his pants. "Gloria," he mumbled in his false sleep. "Oh Gloria...yes...."

Jorge and the other man across from Bolan began to laugh. "He is having a wet dream!" the slender man wearing a green drill instructor's cap said. "Give me some of that drug!" the man shouted.

"Silencio!" Gonzales said.

Bolan used the diversion to slump down farther against the side of the van. His own hands moved to a position just above his waistband. He had only worked with Paul Wilson for a short time but had found the man to be alert and perceptive. More importantly, there was already a certain mental connection between the two men that usually took partners weeks, if not years, to develop. Bolan suspected that the retired Ranger was thinking the same thing he was—that the moment they slowed to go into the mine was the time to strike. He knew for certain that he could count on Wilson to act as soon as he saw the Executioner go into action.

"We are here," the driver said over his shoulder.

The van began to slow.

8

Everyone called him Pepe. He liked the name. But Carlos Gomez-Garcia rarely thought of himself by that appellation. Except on those days when the number after the name was about to change.

And this was one of those days

Pepe 88 took a sip of the strong espresso Juan had just brought him and looked out from the open patio. The house sat high on the side of a mountain, and below he could see the dense jungle of Colombia. Hidden behind the trees and vines, he knew the jaguars lay sleeping, resting up before their nightly hunt for food. Often, long after the sun had fallen, he could look out from this same patio and catch glimpses of their yellow eyes shining in the darkness.

Another sip of espresso turned his thoughts to the past, and Pepe 88 thought of his childhood. His was not a "rags to riches" story like many men in his profession. He had been born the son of a coffee magnate, and grown up on his father's plantation not so many miles from where he sat. His father had always told him he was lazy and worthless because he preferred spending his time with books and his own thoughts rather than working in the coffee fields and learning the family business.

Pepe laughed softly, remembering the old man. He supposed his father's disdain had been at least part of the reason he had joined the FARC movement years ago. Not that he hadn't believed in revolution—he had in those days. But he had also wanted to prove to his father that he had thoughts and ideas of his own, and that he could become successful in areas other than coffee production.

Nine-tenths of every peso earned by Colombian coffee somehow found its way into the pockets of the *norteamericanos*. His father had accepted that as part of conducting a successful business in a Third World country, and never stopped to consider the immorality of it all. Little Carlito—as his mother called him—however, had been determined to reverse that ratio if not eliminate the *yanquis* from the equation completely.

How naive he had been to think he could change a nation. He'd learned it was a task no less daunting than changing basic human nature. It simply could not be done.

Juan appeared in his white jacket and apron, bringing another demitasse of espresso and setting it on the table in front of Pepe 88. The servant did not speak—just frowned quizzically at his master, letting his face ask the question, "Will there be anything else?"

Pepe 88 shook his head and the man disappeared back into the mountainside mansion.

A bird flew overhead and Pepe looked at the sky. It had been several weeks since the Black Hawk helicopters had come, bringing with them the Colombian army or police, but never both. The two factions of the government were in competition with each other. They rarely shared information and *never* shared command. Each wanted to be the one who brought him down so they could brag to the *yanquis* and shout out, "See! We are doing our part! We are doing everything we can to stop the cocaine entering your country to feed the habits of your nation of addicts!"

The thought brought a quiet laugh to Pepe's lips. No, there had not been an attempt to capture him for some time. So the helicopters were due. But he knew there was no reason to worry. He always received plenty of advance warning, and the escape route for him and his men had yet to fail.

Pepe reached into his shirt pocket and pulled out a short, stubby, Cuban cigar. Carefully twisting it in his mouth, he lit the end with a solid gold lighter and sat back in his chair. The nicotine, combined with the caffeine in the espresso, was hitting his system now and giving him the only buzz he ever allowed himself. He never touched any of the products he sold to others. He had seen far too many powerful men brought down by developing such tastes. He even abstained from that most simple of drugs, alcohol.

Next to the ashtray and espresso cup on the glass table in front of him lay a simple wooden handled machete. Pepe left the cigar in his mouth and lifted it with one hand, checking the edge with the other. This simple working blade fascinated him almost as much as the more elaborate machetes that hung on the wall in his office.

He thought of his vast collection. Some bore handles of turquoise, diamonds and gold or silver or both. Others had beautifully patterned Damascus blades. He had been an afficionado of the machete since he'd first seen one as a child. He'd spent many hours perfecting his technique with this most basic of tools. He could throw a machete with accuracy and make it stick at any range—an ability few men had mastered with a weapon primarily designed for chopping. And he could crack open a ripe coconut, and have a piece in his mouth, in less than two seconds.

Pepe took another sip of espresso, puffed on his cigar and chuckled. He often executed this party trick at the functions he sponsored here at his mountain mansion. With it, he had amazed and delighted many of the more affluent men and women in Colombia.

His smile gradually relaxed into a face devoid of emotion. In addition to his party tricks and throwing ability, he had, of course, killed men with machetes. Eighty-eight of them, to be exact.

But that number would soon rise to eighty-nine.

Pepe heard a door open behind him. A moment later a beautiful blond American woman came onto the patio wearing nothing but the bottom part of a thong bikini. She smiled, and her breasts and buttocks bounced invitingly with every step she took toward him.

Pepe smiled again. He had met Michelle three days earlier at one of those very parties at which he had performed his coconut trick, and she had stayed at the mansion. He could tell she was fascinated by him—not only his money and looks but the danger and violence that surrounded his every move. Many women were attracted by such danger, he had learned over the years.

"Good morning, my love," Pepe said as the woman spread a towel on the tiles a few feet from the table and lay down on her back.

"Good morning," Michelle answered, wrapping a pair of sunglasses around her face. "You were wonderful last night, by the way."

Pepe ignored the compliment. He expected such

praise from the women who stayed at the mansion. Sooner of later, he knew, Michelle would be gone. But there would always be another to take her place. "Are you certain you want to tan yourself here this morning?" he asked, puffing away on his cigar. "I believe I told you last night what is going to happen today."

Michelle's expression turned sultry and the skin of her face flushed slightly. "Yes," she said in a husky voice. "You told me. But I have never witnessed anything like that. I want to see it."

Pepe shrugged, staring briefly at her breasts. They were a shade whiter than the rest of her skin and, several shades lighter than his own dark brown. Americans, he thought, shaking his head as he contemplated one of that country's more confusing contradictions. America was a nation that looked down on dark-skinned people of all races. Yet they spent countless hours in the sun trying to make their own skin darker, and seemed to see no incongruity in such behavior.

Juan appeared once more, coming out of the same door Michelle had exited but ignoring the almost nude woman on the tiles. Stopping at the side of the table, the servant said simply, "They are here."

"Then show them out, Juan," Pepe said. "By all means, show them out."

Pepe waited for the three men he knew were about to appear. Two of them—Antonio and Jaime—knew what was about to happen.

Julio did not.

Pepe's three top lieutenants appeared on the patio, led by Juan. While the servant disappeared, all three shot quick glances at Michelle, then turned their eyes to their leader.

Pepe smiled to himself. The 28th Front still put on a

show of being revolutionaries who sold cocaine and kidnapped wealthy men for ransom only to finance their acts
of violence against the Colombian and American govern-
ments. But long ago, revolution had ceased to be Pepe's
goal. The money brought in by the drugs and abductions
had taught him a new respect for capitalism, and he and
his men—while they would never admit it out loud—
lived for the lifestyles such free enterprise provided.

Truly, Pepe thought, the tail had begun to wag the
dog. But he liked it that way. And so did the other men
under his command—some too much.

His three lieutenants took seats around the table.
Julio, seated just to his right at the table, had become
too greedy. In spite of the kindness Pepe had shown him,
the man had begun skimming drugs to sell on his own.

Pepe shook his head in dismay. He and Julio had
been friends since their youth, and while he lacked the
qualities to be a leader, Julio had always been one of the
best *segundos*. He was sorry for what he had to do now.
But if he allowed his friend to get away with stealing
from him, soon everyone in the organization would believe it was acceptable.

The 28th Front leader decided to waste no time.
"Julio," he said. "How are your friends in Miami?"

"Excuse me?" Julio said. He was a big man—well
over six feet tall and at least fifty pounds overweight.
He wore a thin mustache on his plump upper lip, and it
quivered slightly as he spoke. "I am not certain I understand you, Pepe."

"Oh, of course you do," Pepe said. "Your friends in
Miami. The ones of whom you think I am unaware. The
ones who buy the cocaine and heroin you steal from me."

"Pepe," Julio said, shifting his bulky weight uneasily

in the chair, "I am sorry—I do not know where you got this information. But it is false."

From of the corner of his eye, Pepe saw Michelle rise on her elbows to get a better view of the table.

"Julio," Pepe said, then made a clicking sound with his tongue. "You disappoint me, old friend." He paused as tears began to run down the fat man's cheeks, a little surprised when he felt no sympathy whatsoever for his lifelong acquaintance. "Had you come to me and said, 'Pepe, I need more money,' I would have given it to you. You know that, don't you?"

Julio was weeping. "Yes," he said, as snot began to run from his nose onto his upper lip.

The disgusting sight brought a sudden anger to Pepe's heart. But it was having a different effect on Michelle, he could see in his peripheral vision. The woman was breathing harder, her naked breasts heaving on her chest.

Pepe forced himself to hide his disgust with Julio's cowardly behavior. "Do you promise never to do it again?" he asked.

The fat man fell out of his chair onto his knees. Facedown, he reached out and grabbed his boss's hand. "I promise! Oh, Pepe," he cried. "I am sorry. I do not know why I did it. I just…it seemed different at the time. It didn't feel like stealing." His eyes still down, he slobbered kisses over Pepe's hand, which angered the man even further.

"Enough sniveling, old friend," Pepe forced himself to say in a lighthearted voice. "I believe you. But I think you will need my help in keeping your promise never to steal from me again."

Julio still held Pepe's right hand, but the drug lord was as good with his left as his right when manipulating a machete. Suddenly, in one lightninglike motion, he grabbed the handle of the long thin blade from the glass-topped table and raised it high over his head. Then, in one clean and powerful stroke, he brought the razor-honed edge down across the back of Julio's fat neck.

For a second, nothing happened. Then a thin red line appeared on the back of Julio's neck as if someone had circled it with a red pen. A moment later, Julio's head fell from his neck. A jet spray of blood shot out of the stump atop the man's shoulders.

Pepe leaned to the side to avoid the spray, kicking the man's corpse away at the same time. Blood splattered over the short retaining wall that circled the patio. But not a drop touched the leader of the FARC 28th Front.

Pepe stood up. Antonio and Jaime followed him. Pepe stared at both men and the threat was implicit in his eyes.

This is what happens to those who steal from me.

"Will there be anything else, Pepe?" Antonio asked nervously.

The FARC leader shook his head. "Not at the moment. But ask Juan to bring a bucket and mop when you pass back through the house. When he is finished, dump this tub of lard in the jungle."

Jaime smiled nervously. "The jaguars will grow fat tonight," he said as both men made their way toward the door.

As they disappeared into the house, Pepe turned his attention back to the woman on the towel.

"My dear," Pepe said. He stepped to her side and held out a hand, helping her to her feet.

Michelle's eyes stayed riveted on the corpse as they walked toward the house. "You are a truly amazing man, Pepe 88," the blond woman said.

"Yes," he said. "I am. But you are mistaken on one point."

Michelle tore her eyes away from the blood on the patio and stared up into his. "And what is that?" she asked curiously.

"I am no longer Pepe 88," Garcia-Gomez said. "I am now Pepe 89."

9

The van had slowed to around twenty miles per hour when Bolan suddenly stared at the back of the vehicle— at nothing in particular—and shouted out, "What the—"

Even combined with all of the other subtle psychological suggestions that he and Wilson had implanted in the AUC men's minds, the distraction gained the warrior only a split second advantage.

But for a man like the Executioner, a split second was all that was needed.

Shoving his handcuffed hands down inside his waistband with all his strength, Bolan felt the front two belt loops on his pants rip away. His fingertips found the grips of the tiny Guardian where he'd hidden it in his underwear and, a second later, the tiny-but-man-stopping .380 was out of his pants and in action.

At the same time, Wilson drew the .22 Magnum Black Widow.

The Executioner gripped his miniature pistol in both of his handcuffed hands and aimed it at the tall man. To his side, he heard the retired Ranger cock the hammer on the little single-action revolver.

Both guns exploded at the same time.

The sound threatened to break all eardrums inside the

confined area of the van. The Executioner's shot took Gonzales directly through the bridge of the nose and he died never even knowing that he'd been shot.

Wilson's shot drilled into Jorge's temple. The highly penetrating round blasted out the back of Jorge's head, leaving a gaping crater five times the size of the entry hole.

Jorge, too, was out of the action before he even knew what had hit him.

As the Executioner swung the tiny pistol toward the final man guarding them, he heard Wilson cock the mini-revolver once more. By then, however, he had already double-tapped the AUC terrorist, with hollowpoint rounds striking his target in the upper chest and throat. But the green-clad man's senses did not shut down as immediately as those of his head-shot brethren, and as a shower of crimson blasted from both his heart and jugular vein, his trigger finger jerked back on the AK-47 in his hands.

As 7.62 mm rounds began to explode from the Soviet assault rifle, most of them went into the ceiling of the van.

Knowing that the point of aim might change with the next involuntary muscle twitch of the dying man, Bolan took more careful aim and planted another round between the man's eyebrows.

Wilson had crawled through the mayhem, and rose high enough to put a .22 Magnum round into the back of the head of the AUC man riding shotgun for the driver.

Bolan brought both hands back to his waist, then shot them forward with all of the strength in his arms and shoulders. The belt, which had already torn the front loops from his pants, ripped through the buckle behind him. The long piece of leather was still hanging from the chain between his hands as he twisted his pistol until the barrel pointed directly back at his face.

Such a maneuver violated every rule of gun safety and every shooting law taught on police and military gun ranges the world over. But the Executioner knew that true combat had about as much to do with what you learned on the firing range as what you could learn playing golf or table tennis. The ruling god of close quarters combat was Chaos and, when your life and the lives of other innocents were on the line, nothing went quite the way you'd been taught it would.

The Executioner kept his thumb out of the trigger guard as he looped his bound hands up and over the head of the man behind the wheel of the van. Then, with the little .380 still in both hands, he twisted his left forearm into the driver's throat and executed a makeshift version of the time-proved sleeper hold.

The difference was that the Guardian was now pressed into the driver's right eye socket. And Bolan's thumb rode the trigger, ready to curl back and blast a hole through the AUC driver's skull.

Bolan leaned to the side in case the round penetrated the driver's head. Pressing the underside of his forearm into the man's windpipe, he yelled, "Stop the van!" But the driver had been doing that already— slowing the vehicle even before the action behind him had broken out. And the entire gun battle had taken only three-to-five seconds. Still in shock, what was actually happening had not yet had time to sink into his brain.

The driver didn't hesitate in removing his foot from the accelerator and driving it into the brake pedal. As the tires screamed, skidding the van to a halt, the Executioner looked through the windshield. In the moonlight, he could just make out a gaping black hole in the mountain ahead. He squinted. What he was seeing had to be the entrance to the abandoned salt mine.

"Get out, go around the van and open the driver's door," Bolan instructed Wilson. The retired Ranger slid the door to their side open and did just that.

Now," Bolan said, "shake this guy down. Make sure he doesn't have any weapons. I'll join you in a minute." He raised his handcuffed wrists from around the man's throat, regripped the pistol properly, then climbed out of the van himself.

By the time he had joined Wilson the man had taken a Colt Python from the driver's belt. Switching the Black Widow to his left hand, he swung the revolver's cylinder open to make sure it was fully loaded, then closed it again. He had also found the surviving AUC man's key ring. Hidden between larger keys was one that unlocked the handcuffs. Leaning over, he released Bolan's wrists.

The driver, who was clean shaved and looked to be several years older than the others—probably in his early forties—still sat sideways on the seat, the door between him, Bolan and Wilson.

"This where you've kept other hostages?" Bolan demanded, indicating the dark entrance to the mine with a nod of his head.

The AUC man snarled in contempt. But even in the dim light, the Executioner could see the fear in his eyes.

"We didn't come after you AUC guys tonight," Bolan said. "We were trying to make contact with Pepe 88's FARC 28th Front. You know anything about them?"

The driver spit.

Bolan shoved the muzzle of the Guardian up to the man's cheek, just below one of his frightened eyes. "I don't like having to repeat myself. So answer my question before you find yourself with serious sinus problems. Do you know anything about Carlos Gomez-Garcia, the man they call Pepe 88?"

"No," the AUC man said. "We have nothing to do with Communist scum like him. Or you."

Wilson let the ribbed barrel of the AUC man's own Colt Python fall on the cheek opposite where Bolan's Guardian still rested. "We aren't Communists. In fact we're here to kill as many of them as we can on our way to finding Pepe 88. But we don't mind offing a few of you fascist sons of bitches along the way," he said.

"Is there anything you can tell us about Pepe 88?" Bolan asked again.

But the driver just spit again. "The only thing I know is that, as of earlier this morning, he is now called Pepe 89."

Bolan frowned. "He killed someone else with his machete? Who?"

The driver shrugged. "Who knows for sure. It was only a rumor. But the story is that it was one of his own top men."

"And that's all you can tell us about him?" Bolan asked.

The driver nodded.

"Then I guess we don't have any more use for you," Wilson said.

"Tell me," Bolan said. "When we go into that mine in a few minutes, how many bodies of innocent people are we going to find?"

A perverse pride within the AUC man's soul brought on a sudden reckless courage. Bolan watched the look in the man's eyes change from fear to intense hatred. "Many," he said, sticking his chin out in defiance. "And many I have killed with my own hand." The man lunged.

The .357 Magnum contact shot practically destroyed the terrorist's face, drilling through his cheek and into his brain where its semijacketed hollowpoint disintegrated into pieces. Gray matter, blood and other body fluids splattered the windshield and door window of the van as the AUC driver fell back across the seat behind him. Wilson jammed the Python into his belt, then lowered the hammer on the minirevolver in his other hand to half-cock. Twisting the cylinder slightly, he let the hammer fall into one of the safety grooves between the chambers. Reaching forward, he opened the door, grabbed the dead terrorist's ankles and slid him from the van onto the ground. "You realize this van is our only ride back to town, don't you?" he said.

Bolan walked around the van and opened the passenger's door. As he'd suspected he would, he found a flashlight in the glove compartment. "Well," he told the blacksuit-trained Ranger, "you made the mess. So you get to clean it up."

"Thanks a lot," Wilson muttered.

"While you do that I'll carry these bodies into the mine. I doubt anyone will come along here. But there's no sense in leaving evidence out in the open when we don't have to." Without another word, he flipped on the flashlight and walked around to the van's sliding door. Then, as Wilson began his cleanup, Bolan carried the dead terrorists, one by one, into the black hole in the distance.

By the time Bolan returned to the outside world he could see by the moonlight that Wilson had done a fair job of cleaning up the van. "Gee, that was fun," he said as Bolan approached. "Give me as many jobs like that as you can, okay?"

Bolan nodded in the darkness but didn't answer. He noted that the retired Texas Ranger had found a pair of leather work gloves somewhere in the vehicle, and watched as the man carefully removed them now, making sure none of the blood and other fluids got on his hands or arms.

Wilson had piled the AUC men's weapons next to the sliding door of the van, along with all of the extra magazines and ammunition he had found in the vehicle. A sawed-off shotgun was on the top of the heap, and the retired Ranger scooped it up. "You want this thing?" he asked the Executioner.

Bolan reached down and pulled one of the AK-47s from the pile as he shook his head. "No," he said. "This'll do me just fine."

"Good," Wilson said. "'Cause I always sorta favored these stubbies." He pulled a nylon bandolier filled with 12-gauge shells from the stack and slid it over his shoulder before breaking open the double-barreled weapon to be sure it was loaded. Together, the two men tossed the rest of the rifles, extra magazines and other paraphernalia into the rear of the van before Bolan slid the door closed once more.

The Executioner got behind the wheel. Wilson settled into the passenger seat. There were still traces of blood here and there. Several bullet holes were visible in the van's side panels, but nothing had broken the tinted side windows or windshield, and most had gone through the roof where they would not be noticeable. Bolan doubted anyone would even give the bullet holes a second look. In Colombia, bullet holes in a vehicle were almost as common as bug spots on the windshield.

As they headed toward the city, Wilson turned slightly in his seat. "So," he said, "what's next?"

Bolan shook his head. "I don't know yet," he said. "We're pretty much back to square one. But give me the ride back to town to think about everything. I'll come up with something."

"Oh, I'm sure you will," Wilson said. He rested the sawed-off shotgun across his lap, the barrels aimed away from the Executioner.

10

Dawn was breaking by the time the van pulled off the highway onto the road leading to the jungle cottage Wilson had rented. Bolan had driven them from the abandoned salt mine to Bogotá, then the retired Ranger had taken the wheel. This had given both men the opportunity to doze off for some much needed sleep.

Wilson parked the van in front of the small hut, and he and Bolan carried their new arsenal up the steps. Dumping it all in the middle of the one-room shack, they took seats on the floor and began taking inventory.

None of the rifles—or the rest of the equipment for that matter—had been particularly well cared for. Rust spots were evident on almost all of the AKs, and much of the ammunition in the metal ammo boxes had corroded. They went through every round, dividing the good from the bad with a third category of maybes. They would use these to test fire the rifles, and if they encountered any problems only then would they burn up the good rounds in order to determine whether the problem was in the weapon or ammunition.

That would, of course, cut into their stockpile, but only a fool would let his life depend on guns or cartridges he hadn't fired sufficiently to have faith. The

Executioner would rather go into battle with a single-shot .22 than a more powerful, higher capacity weapon with questionable reliability.

Breaking down all of the rifles first, Bolan and Wilson went to work inspecting each part. They needed only one weapon apiece, and by cannibalizing unbroken parts they came up with a pair that might not have won any shooting medals but could be counted on to do what an AK-47 was designed to do.

Kill men.

"Anybody around close enough to hear us test fire?" Bolan asked.

Wilson shook his head. "Not supposed to be another cottage for several miles," he said. "But even if they hear the rounds go off, so what? I mean, this *is* Colombia, after all. People shooting guns and getting shot is so common most people just block it out of their hearing anyway."

"Good point," Bolan said and stood up. "You happen to bring along any hearing protectors?"

The blacksuit-trained man shook his head. "No," he said. "Didn't occur to me we would be spending any time at a firing range. But I've got a box of cotton in my first-aid kit."

"Bring it," the Executioner said as he slung one of the good AK-47s over his shoulder. He dropped all of the extra magazines into one of Wilson's larger duffels as the retired Ranger dumped the divided piles of ammo into three smaller bags.

Bolan led the way down the steps to the side of the house. Together, the two men began the laborious chore of loading the magazines with the "maybe" rounds. When all the boxes were full, Wilson pulled a wad of cotton from his back pocket and tore it in two, handing one to the Executioner.

Bolan tore it again, stuffing a white ball into each ear. In the heat of battle, no one could afford to stop and put on ear protectors of any kind. But there was no sense risking your own hearing when you didn't have to.

Wilson had found a few white paper plates in the cottage and he walked deeper into the jungle carrying them. The foliage was so thick there would be no chance to test fire for long-range accuracy—just short-range reliability. The retired Ranger was no more than twenty yards away when he turned around. "This looks like the longest open stretch we're gonna get," he said, shaking his head.

"Put 'em up then," Bolan said.

Wilson broke a limb from one of the trees at roughly head level. Then, carefully, he pushed the paper plate through the sharp end still attached to the trunk. Hanging two more paper plates, the retired Ranger walked back to where Bolan stood waiting.

"Take the one on your side," the Executioner said. "We need to check every magazine. If you have a misfire put in a round we know is still good. If it misfires again, chuck the magazine. At the end of the testing, we'll run several of the rounds we know are still good through each mag."

"And what if it still keeps jamming?" Wilson asked.

"Then it's time to get rid of the rifle itself and go back to your girlfriends, Betty and Becky."

Bolan was pleasantly surprised to find that much of the uncertain ammunition could still be fired, and all but one of the magazines in his stack worked without flaw. Wilson was almost as lucky, having to dump only two magazines and surprised to find that his AK-47—always known more for reliability than accuracy, could keep the rounds in a tight half-inch group at the twenty-odd yards they were firing.

Satisfied that they'd separated the good from the bad, and the ugly, both men pulled the cotton from their ears.

"Your Explorer is still at that shopping mall back in the city," Bolan said as they walked back toward the cottage. "We'll leave it where it is and use the van as long as we can."

Wilson nodded as they walked up the steps. "There'll be thousands of vans just like it in a city the size of Bogotá," he agreed. "Might as well take advantage of that fact until it gets burned."

Bolan opened the door to the cottage on stilts and ushered Wilson in ahead of him. The two men leaned their rifles against the wall and lay the extra magazines—now fully loaded with the reliable ammo—on the floor next to them before taking seats at the table.

Wilson reached into his seemingly endless line of soft-sided luggage and pulled out a gallon bottle of Gatorade and two plastic cups. He poured two drinks before sitting down. "So," he said, leaning back. "We got a new plan yet?"

Bolan nodded. "I've been thinking about it ever since we left the salt mine," he said. "We've been going about this backwards. What we need to do is become the kidnappers and snatch up a FARC hardman," he stated.

Wilson frowned. "How do you plan to do that? I mean, how are we going to know Pepe's men from the other thousands of street toughs and terrorists in this town?"

Bolan looked down at the intelligence file which was still on the table. But before he could speak, Wilson went on.

"Yeah, sure," he said. "We've got photos of some of his top guys. But what did you have in mind? Going back and showing them at every cantina in town? Believe me, no amount of reward money is going to get anyone to rat them out. Everyone is too afraid of Pepe and the rest of his organization."

Bolan nodded. "That wasn't what I had in mind at all," he said.

"Well, then tell me what you *do* have on your mind," the retired Ranger said. "Because these guys don't walk around wearing signs that say, *I'm a FARC. Please kidnap me*. It'll be like looking for needle in a haystack."

"Agreed," the Executioner said. "Which is why we need to get the haystack raked down as small as possible before we begin."

"And how do you plan to do that?"

"By doing something I should have done before we went out trying to get kidnapped," Bolan said. He reached behind him to his new suit jacket, which had been hung over the back of his chair, and pulled his cell phone out of the inside breast pocket. Flipping the instrument open, he turned it on.

The phone took a few seconds to warm up. Wilson said, "Oh, I see, you're just going to call the FARC information hot line." He slapped himself on the forehead. "Why didn't I think of that?"

When the cell phone was up and running, Bolan engaged the scrambling device on his end before tapping in the direct number to Stony Man Farm. He waited as the call bounced off nine dummy numbers on three different continents before finally reaching the Farm.

"Hello, Striker," Barbara Price said after the first ring. "How's your tropical vacation going?"

Bolan laughed, at the same time forming a mental picture of the woman at the mission control desk. Barbara Price was living proof that women could be competent, top-rate professionals and still have the looks of an international supermodel.

"Well," the Executioner said, "the weather's nice. And it's nice and quiet. At least where I am right now.'

"I'll bet it hasn't been that way the whole time," Price said, and this time her tone of voice revealed no mirth.

"There's been a little excitement," Bolan said. "I'll tell you all about it when we get time. Is the Bear handy?" Bolan asked.

"Hang loose," Price said. "I'll put you through."

As the Executioner waited for the line to connect, Wilson said, "The Bear. Big man in a wheelchair, right? The one who plays the computer the way Liberace played the piano?"

Bolan only had time to nod before Aaron Kurtzman, Stony Man Farm's resident computer genius, said, "What can I do for you, big guy?"

"You can tap into all of the police and military intelligence files for Colombia," Bolan said. "I need to know places where known FARCs hang out. Especially any FARCs with the 28th Front."

"Pepe 88's bunch, you mean?" Kurtzman asked.

"Yeah," the Executioner said. "Except that now I understand he's become Pepe 89."

"Give me a minute and let me see what I can do," Kurtzman said.

Bolan looked at his wristwatch, his mind on the man in the wheelchair. No one could hack into the files of an enemy faster or more efficiently than Kurtzman.

Instead of the minute he'd asked for, Kurtzman was

back in thirty seconds. "I've got a list of a little over a dozen places," he said. "Want me to give them all to you?"

Bolan felt his eyebrows lower in thought. "Are they listed in order of preference?" Bolan asked. "I mean, like which the FARCs frequent most?"

There was a short pause, then Kurtzman said, "Doesn't look like it. They're alphabetical."

The Executioner paused. He didn't have time to play hit or miss with over a dozen of Bogotá's dives. "Is there a way, Bear," he finally said, "for you to run these places back through your magic machines and list them in order of likelihood?"

"Sure," Kurtzman said. "All I have to do is program in the names and see which ones show up most frequently in the intelligence and incident reports. Give me another minute."

On the other end of the line, Bolan could hear the computer wizard tapping the keys. "Okay, Striker," he said. "You prepared to copy?"

Wilson had anticipated the need to write and had already pulled a pen and notepad out of his baggage. He extended them to Bolan now.

Kurtzman read. Bolan wrote. And a few minutes later the Executioner had the names of fourteen places known to be FARC hangouts—in the order that was most likely to find them a terrorist.

"Thanks a million, Bear," Bolan said.

"Anytime, Striker," Kurtzman replied. "After all, that's what they pay me the big bucks to do."

Bolan hung up, dropped the phone back into his jacket pocket and stood up.

Wilson stood up with him. "You got the names of the places these guys frequent, I take it?" he said.

The Executioner nodded. "Let's change clothes and get on the road."

Wilson reached into one of the bags and pulled out a clean pair of blue jeans, a white T-shirt and a batik print short-sleeved shirt, tossing them to Bolan. Reaching in again, he found similar clothing for himself. He grinned at the Executioner. "Glad to get out of this monkey suit, to tell you the truth," he said. "It just didn't look right with my Ranger hat."

11

The Cascabel Grande was not exactly what could be called an upscale night club. On the other hand, it was a far cry from the sleazy dives Bolan and Wilson had gone to during their earlier attempts to find members of FARC's 28th Front. Dress was casual, and the jeans, T-shirts, and even Wilson's Texas Ranger cowboy hat would fit in perfectly when they finally went in.

But, after two hours of waiting in the van, parked on the street across and down the block from the front door, the Executioner wasn't sure this battle plan was going to work out any better than the earlier ones.

Bolan and Wilson sat quietly, the Executioner behind the wheel. They had circled the building once, finding that the rear of the club had one exit door and three windows. One of the windows was large and dropped down to knee level, so that even though what lay behind it was hidden by venetian blinds, Bolan had to guess it led to an office area. The other two windows were much smaller and set far higher in the wall. Wilson had hopped out of the van long enough to jump up and catch a glimpse through both. One window led out from the ladies' restroom. The other led out from the men's.

Their reconnaissance accomplished, they had parked

the bullet-pocked AUC van where they could see both
the front door and parking lot but would not be noticeable themselves. Then they had watched the single
men, couples, and larger groups come and go. Wilson
had chuckled at the name of the club.

Cascabel grande, meant "big poisonous snake."

But so far, Bolan and his partner had not been able
to ID any of the FARC 28th Front snakes from the photos in the intelligence file that lay open on the seat
between them. They wanted to be sure before picking
someone to nab. They had already spent too much time
looking in the wrong directions. Luck had not been with
them—but that was just how it went sometimes.

A late model Cadillac turned into the parking lot and
disappeared toward the rear of the lot. A few moments
later, a middle-aged man, overdressed for the club in an
expensive gray pinstripe suit and Gucci loafers, escorted
a woman young enough to be his daughter out of the
darkness under the light in front of the club. Bolan studied the man's face. He had a long scar running from just
above the left ear down to his chin, and it looked like it
had been put there by a knife of some sort. He wore
a very good expensive, toupee—but it was a toupee
nonetheless. The Executioner's sensors perked into high
gear, and he looked down at the photos spread out on
the bench seat between him and Wilson. The man's
scarred face didn't match up to any of the pictures so
there was no way to know if he was FARC or just
another of the thousands of unaffiliated outlaws who
called Bogotá home.

But the Executioner's gut told him the man was well
worth keeping in mind.

Another thirty minutes went by with other men and women arriving and leaving. But none even came close to matching up to the photos. Wilson had just said, "You don't suppose you could call the Farm and see if that Bear guy has any other pics—" when a BMW similar to the one Bolan had abandoned earlier drove into the lot.

Bolan held up a hand to silence his partner as a tall, gangly man exited the vehicle. He wore white slacks, white shoes and a white shirt. He checked his long curly hair in the side mirror of the BMW, then started for the door to the club. Every few feet he broke out into some kind of dance move, then strutted on until he felt the urge to shake and shimmy again.

"I could show you saloons in Texas where they'd kill that son of a bitch just for walking like that," Wilson said. "And it'd probably get ruled justifiable homicide."

Bolan had felt the hair on the back of his neck rise as soon as he'd caught the first glimpse of the man's face. Though he still hadn't gotten a good enough look to be certain, his instincts told him they were finally on to something.

"No," he said, finally answering Wilson. "If the Bear had any more pictures, we'd already have them ourselves. But take a close look at this string-bean fellow when he dances his way under the light above the door. I think this may be one of our men."

The man pranced his way into the light, then he turned his curly head toward the van and looked almost directly at where Bolan and Wilson sat watching.

"You're right as rain," the retired Ranger said as Bolan reached down and began shuffling through the photos, a mini flashlight clamped between his teeth. He found the photo he was looking for and turned it so both he and his partner could see it.

The only difference in the face across the street and the one looking up from the seat was that the dancer had grown his hair a little longer and had a few more wrinkles in his face, which had come with age.

"Bingo. I believe we've done found us a turkey to shoot."

"What's his name?" Wilson asked as the FARC man disappeared into the club.

"Heredia," Bolan said, squinting at the words beneath the photograph of the man. "Frederico Heredia." He looked up in time to see Heredia disappear into the club. "Was he looking at us or just in this general direction?"

"He didn't seem to be paying any attention to us if he saw us," Wilson said. "I get the idea he was *posing* in case someone might be watching. Or maybe the little peacock caught another reflection of himself in a window or something."

Bolan handed Heredia's picture to Wilson for a closer look, took the flashlight out of his mouth and directed the beam on the brief intel report that came next in the file. "He seems to be middle management," he said, scanning the page. "Started out as rank and file FARC, then specialized in single assassinations." He paused, frowning, as he reached the end of the report.

Wilson saw the frown and said, "What's wrong?"

"He's listed here as being with the 14th Front," Bolan said.

"You ask me," Wilson said. "that's maybe the closest we're going to get on this rabbit hunt. We been sitting here for two hours and that's the only guy we've been able to positively ID yet as a FARC of any sort."

Bolan nodded his head. "You're right," he said. "We may have to play leapfrog to get to Pepe 88 or 89 or whatever his number is by now. But at least this is a start." He opened the door to the van and got out. Before closing it, he leaned back in. "Stick to the original plan. Give me five minutes before you come in."

"That's a big 10-4," Wilson said. As Bolan closed the door the man reached for his Ranger hat and set it on his head, adjusting it to the angle he preferred.

Bolan took a deep breath as he walked across the street. And as he walked, he patted himself down, making sure that the Beretta, Desert Eagle, TOPS SAW knife and the little Guardian were all in place. Somewhere, deep in the back of his mind, he barely registered the fact that he looked like a man trying to remember which pocket he'd put his cigarettes in.

Over the years, covering such actions as double-checking his weapons had become second nature to him. And as long as everything went according to plan, he wouldn't need a gun or knife of any sort during his time inside the Cascabel Grande.

But things didn't always go according to plan.

BOLAN SPOTTED the only empty table in the place and took a seat. He couldn't have hoped for a better spot. His back was against the wall, he had a view of both the front door and the men's room and could also see the dance floor and the tables in between.

The first thing he noticed as he sat down was the familiar feeling that the place just wasn't right. It was an instinct he'd learned to trust over the years.

A waitress wearing a bad attempt at a bunny costume, sans ears, strutted over and smiled down at

Bolan. "What I can get for you, my big friend?" she asked in broken English.

Bolan ordered a beer. The woman herself was far more attractive than her costume, and as she walked away he felt eyes on him. He threw a quick glance around the room and saw that this feeling was not without basis. Several of the tougher looking men in the place were looking his way, wondering who this new gringo might be.

Bolan turned his attention to the bandstand beyond the dance floor, where the mediocre musicians were playing a combination of tangos, rumbas and other music. He didn't want trouble with anyone besides Heredia—it would do nothing but slow down his quest to find Pepe. But he knew that the men looking him over had also developed their instincts for trouble. And they sensed the same potential for violence in him that he did in them.

The waitress brought the beer and opened it at the table. Then, wiggling her half-bare hips provocatively, she walked away again. Bolan took a sip, then set the bottle back on the table in front of him.

When Bolan finally glanced around the room again, the men who had stared at him earlier had gone back to whatever they'd been doing before he walked in. Whatever it was the gringo was up to, they wanted no more part of it than he wanted to get sidetracked by them.

Without being asked, the waitress brought the Executioner another beer. As she set it on the table next to the one he still had, she smiled invitingly. Getting no response for her effort, she walked away again, the disappointment apparent on her face.

Bolan took another sip of the first beer as Wilson walked in.

The Executioner watched his partner as the man made his way to a stool at the bar. There were at least two dozen other straw cowboy hats scattered throughout the tables and the dance floor, and the drummer for the band wore one. The ex-Ranger didn't look any more out of place than Bolan.

Frederico Heredia was sitting at a table filled with hard-looking women and men, and doing his best to hit on the woman sitting next to him. She was very attractive, and Bolan certainly couldn't blame the FARC man for trying. He could, however, blame him for just about every other aspect of his despicable life. Sometimes directly, other times indirectly, Heredia had been responsible for the deaths of countless innocent men, women and children.

Bolan finished the first beer but made no move toward the second. Things were about to change for Frederico Heredia.

Out of the corner of his eye, the Executioner watched Wilson order a beer, then turn on his stool to gaze out over the crowd. The waitress attending to the drinks at Heredia's table seemed to catch the Texan's eye for a moment, but Bolan was sure he wouldn't be distracted from the mission for very long.

A few minutes later, Heredia and the woman next to him stood up and headed for the dance floor. The man in white began to dance, hoping to impress his partner with his moves in ways he seemed to have been unable to do with words.

From the bored expression on the woman's face as she danced, the Executioner's guess was that the FARC man was having no more luck on the dance floor than he'd had seated at the table.

Finally, after they had returned to their seats and Heredia had downed several shots and beers, the FARC man's bladder got the best of him. He stood up, pushed his chair back and started weaving his way through the crowd toward the men's room at the back of the club.

Bolan rose and dropped enough money to pay for his beer and leave a substantial tip on the table, then followed. He saw Wilson acting similarly at the bar. They passed each other going in opposite directions, then the Executioner followed Frederico Heredia as Wilson headed out the front door.

A long, stainless-steel trough served as the urinal, running along the right side of the men's room. Heredia was at the far end, and was still jiving to the music blasting in from the other room as he reached with his right hand to lower his zipper.

Bolan took a fast look around and saw that they were the only occupants, then walked up to Heredia's side.

Heredia looked uncomfortable when Bolan stopped right next to him. But the look didn't last long before Bolan's right cross drove into his chin and knocked him unconscious to the floor.

Bolan grabbed the man under the arms and dragged him across the room to the wall beneath the window. He guessed that Wilson had already reached the van. It would be another minute or two before he pulled it around into the alley.

The Executioner looked at the door leading out into the main room of the Cascabel Grande. There was no way to lock it.

Less than thirty seconds after Bolan had put Heredia to sleep, a pudgy man wearing a loud-print polyester shirt wove his way in and up to the urinal, unzipping his skintight double-knit pants. He looked like one of the few faces in the club too soft to be involved in terrorism or crime of any sort, and half proved that to Bolan when he slurred out, "Your friend drinking too much?"

Bolan nodded. The pudgy man's eyes were bloodshot from drinking too much himself, and he continued to weave his weight uncertainly back and forth as he urinated into the metal trough. The Executioner doubted that the man would remember much about this encounter, when he'd sobered up. So there was no reason to add him to the baggage he'd be taking with him.

"He passed out taking a leak," Bolan said offhandedly. "So I thought I'd better let him get a little air by the window before I tried to wake him up."

The man in the skintight pants and wild shirt nodded. "Some guys just can't hold their liquor," he slurred proudly, trying to keep his balance himself.

Bolan forced a laugh of agreement. It was a pretty sure bet that the dumpy man didn't know Heredia, or that he was part of the FARC organization.

The pudgy man finished his business, then walked out without another word.

The Executioner continued to wait, the minutes he knew it was taking Wilson to bring the van around feeling like hours. But he had no other choice except to be patient, and play each new card that was dealt as best he could. If more men entered the restroom, he would have to make instant decisions about what to do with them as he had the man who had just left. But if he was lucky, maybe Wilson would arrive before that happened.

He wasn't that lucky.

The next man through the door had a recognizable

face—but not from the intelligence photos. He was the middle-aged man with the long scar from ear to chin, who Bolan and Wilson had seen earlier. He looked at Bolan, then to Heredia on the floor, and the Executioner knew in a split second that, unlike the fat man before him, he understood what was happening.

Bolan didn't know if the man was FARC or not. But he was certainly savvy enough to go back outside and tell everyone in the club what was happening in the men's room.

But the scar-faced hard case was also smart enough not to show what he sensed. Instead, he said almost the same thing the fat man had said. "Frederico drinks too much," he muttered as if completely disinterested as he walked to the urinal.

If Bolan had had any doubt at all up until this point as to how to handle the scar-faced man, that doubt disappeared with the man's words. The scar-faced man knew Frederico Heredia by name. That meant he knew the man was FARC.

As he rose quickly from the floor and slid catlike toward the urinal, Bolan found himself in the wrong position to employ another of his powerful right crosses. But the left hook that smashed into the scar on the man's jaw seemed to work just as well, and suddenly he had two unconscious men on the floor waiting for Wilson to arrive.

Which, luckily, happened only a few seconds later.

"Cooper!" Bolan heard the retired Ranger whisper through the high window to the alley. "You there?"

"I'm here," Bolan whispered back. "And I've got two coming through to you." As he lifted Heredia from the floor, he got no response from Wilson. Who was smart enough to know that there were times for questions, and other times when speed of action was far more important than understanding sudden details that had changed.

The window was barely large enough to squeeze Heredia through, and reconfirmed the Executioner's good fortune that he had not had to try the same thing with the pudgy man in the loud clothes. Bolan got the FARC man's head and shoulders into the small opening, and then pushed on the legs while Wilson pulled from the outside.

The entire operation took only a few seconds. But by the time he was ready to lift the older man with the facial scar, the victim of Bolan's second punch was stirring. This time, however, the Executioner was in a perfect position for his right cross. Throwing it with all the power in his arm and shoulder at a downward angle, the punch caught the man squarely on the chin and sent him back into the world of dreams.

The middle-aged man was not only shorter, he had of a smaller frame than the white-clad, FARC man, and he went through the window far faster and easier. Bolan didn't waste any time pulling himself up and through the window before dropping down into the alley behind the club.

As his feet hit the ground, the Executioner could see that Wilson already had the side door of the van open. Both of the unconscious men were laid out in the back. Behind him, from the men's room, he heard a voice say in Spanish, "What the hell?"

Whoever was behind the voice had to have caught a glimpse of Bolan dropping from the window. But it was unlikely that whoever it was had recognized the new gringo, or knew that Bolan had shoved two other men out into the alley before him. In any case, the Executioner didn't wait to find out. Hurrying to the open side door of the van, he leaped inside. Then, without turning his face so it could be seen from the restroom window, he reached behind him and slid the door shut again.

Wilson was already behind the wheel and as the door closed he pulled away from the window.

The Executioner looked out through the heavily tinted glass, knowing no one watching would be able to make out his facial features. And there *was* another face staring back at the van from the window. But that face just looked puzzled at what was happening, and Bolan's best guess told him that whoever it was had not seen him, Wilson, or the faces of their prisoners.

At least Bolan hoped that was the case. They were still operating on the hope that while Pepe knew there were American agents on the ground looking for him, the FARC leader had no accurate description of them. At best, he thought Bolan had blond hair and a matching beard. At worst, Pepe might suspect it had been a disguise. But even if the latter was the case, the FARC leader still wouldn't know what the Executioner or the retired Ranger looked like.

And while it didn't matter much at the moment, the Executioner knew that sooner or later, the fact that Pepe had no good descriptions of them was going to become essential.

12

The Executioner had never believed in torture as a method for obtaining information from the enemy. For one thing, it was beneath the dignity of a true warrior. And in a more pragmatic light, it was an ineffectual way of getting what you wanted out of a man.

Under torture, a man would tell you whatever he thought you wanted to hear that would stop the pain. That wasn't always the truth. And what Bolan needed from either, or both, of the men in the van *was* the truth.

On the other hand, while torture itself achieved questionable results, the Executioner had learned during his long career that the *threat* of torture could be quite beneficial. Often, it scared a man into talking before actual pain had driven him past the point where he even knew what the truth was. Fright sometimes brought the words rolling off a tongue as fast as it could move.

Dawn was still an hour or so away when Wilson pulled the van onto the jungle path leading out of sight from the road to the cottage. Both of the men in the back were awake, but long before they had regained consciousness the Executioner had removed their shirts and used the garments as blindfolds.

Bolan studied Heredia as the van slowed, nearing the

cottage. The man was still wearing his white pants and shoes, and was shivering as if it were below zero instead of ninety above in the jungle. As soon as he'd awakened, he had asked where they were, where they were going and who it was with him in the van. But a slap across his shirt-covered face and a growling, "Shut up," from Bolan had silenced him for the rest of the ride.

Turning his attention to the other prisoner, Bolan studied the older man. In contrast to Heredia, he sat passively waiting for whatever was to come. He knew he was in a position he had no control over but that realism didn't seem to bother him, and the Executioner wondered exactly who he was. He had shaken down both men while they'd been unconscious and, while the man with the scar on his face carried a billfold in the right-rear pocket of his slacks, it contained nothing to identify him.

Whoever he was, he was obviously an old hand at this game. And he didn't want anyone knowing his identity unless he chose to expose it.

Again, the Executioner got the sense that this middle-aged man might prove even more valuable than the younger one. But he was also more dangerous, Bolan knew.

The soldier made a decision as the van ground to a halt outside the one-room cottage on stilts. The middle-aged man, his gut told him, should be the one on whom he concentrated. He remembered the man's use of Heredia's name. The fact that he knew the now-quivering man in white meant there was a better than even chance that he had at least some kind of connection to the FARCs, as well.

So Bolan would use Heredia primarily to set up the

older man for questioning. If that line of interrogation proved wrong, he could always drop back, punt and start over again.

But the Executioner didn't think he'd have to do that.

Bolan had ridden in the back of the van to keep an eye on his prisoners. But, as Wilson stopped the vehicle next to the cottage, he leaned over the seat and said, "I'm taking the Dancing King inside to question him. Let me borrow your bowie knife."

The Executioner still had one eye on the men in the rear of the van, and he saw Heredia flinch when he heard the words.

The older man continued to sit passively next to him.

Wilson frowned for a moment, then leaned forward and drew the huge blade from the sheath behind his back. Twirling it in his hand, he extended it to the Executioner.

"Stay here with the other guy," Bolan said, making sure his voice could be heard behind him again. "His time will come as soon as I'm done with Frederico."

Heredia flinched again at the sound of his name. The fact that his captors knew him added to his fear.

With Wilson's big naked blade in one hand, Bolan opened the sliding door with the other, got out, and then jerked Frederico Heredia from the vehicle. The man fell onto the ground, a tiny shriek escaping his lips. Grabbing an arm, Bolan jerked him to his feet and led him to the steps. "Up," he said, pushing the man ahead of him.

Heredia stepped tentatively onto the first step.

"Move!" Bolan shouted into the blindfolded man's ear, and Heredia tried running up the stairs. He stumbled twice before making it to the top, moaning in pain each time a knee hit the sharp wooden steps or he banged an elbow against the rail.

"You think that hurts?" the Executioner asked in a low menacing voice. "Wait until we get inside."

A sniveling sound escaped Heredia's mouth.

When they reached the landing outside the front of the cottage, the Executioner opened the door and shoved his prisoner inside. Heredia tripped over the doorway and fell flat on his face. He'd had his hand handcuffed behind his back, and Bolan reached down, grabbed the chain between his wrists and hoisted him to his feet again. Heredia howled.

Bolan pushed him into the room, still twisting the handcuff chain. It created pain but would do no permanent damage. When they reached the table, the Executioner turned Heredia around and slammed him into one of the chairs. "Sit still," he ordered. "You move a muscle, and I'll kill you right here and now. You understand?"

The man nodded.

Bolan set the bowie knife on the table in front of the still-sightless man, then dug quickly through the bags Wilson had brought along. He found a notebook from which he ripped a single page, then several loops of green paracord held in place by a strip of tape. Unwinding the cord, he used it to tie Heredia to the back of the chair. Then, lifting the huge knife in his right hand, he held it in front of Heredia's face as he ripped the shirt off the man's face with his left.

The glistening steel blade, with the copper strip along the spine, was the first thing the FARC man saw as the shirt came off his face. He froze, staring at his own distorted reflection in the blade.

Bolan pulled the other chair around the table to face Heredia, then sat down knee to knee with the man. He lifted the blank piece of paper he had torn from the notebook and began cutting it into thin strips with the bowie. When all of the strips had fallen to the floor, he extended his left arm and shaved off a short section of hair. Wiping the hair from the knife on his pants leg, he set the bowie in his lap.

The FARC man's eyes had followed the entire demonstration.

"Now," Bolan said, smiling at the man whose face was only a foot or so away. "I don't particularly want to hurt you. But I don't *mind* hurting you if I have to. Do we both understand that?"

A whimper came out of Heredia's mouth as he nodded, his eyes still on the knife.

"Look at me!" Bolan commanded, and Heredia's eyes jerked upward. "I want to know what part you play in the FARC organization, and everything you know about Pepe 89."

"Are you...*policia?*" Heredia managed to whimper out.

Bolan reached down in one lightninglike movement, grabbed the handle of the bowie and slapped Heredia across the cheek with the flat side of the blade. The man's cheek turned instantly red, and a small lump began to swell on the high cheekbone.

"*I'm* the one who asks the questions," Bolan said. "Is that clear?"

Heredia had been more surprised by the strike to the face than hurt. He nodded in understanding, then tried to look at his own cheek with both eyes to see if he'd been cut. The attempt would have been comical had the Executioner not been so disgusted with the cowardly excuse for a man sitting next to him.

This, Bolan knew, was a man who had no problem killing innocent people in the name of his criminal-terrorist organization. It probably didn't bother him a bit when FARC bombs ripped the bodies of children to unidentifiable shreds, or when stray shots from drive-by shootings missed their marks and took out innocent men and women. And Bolan doubted that Heredia had lost a minute's sleep from knowing that the cocaine snorted, the crack smoked, and the heroin mainlined into veins and arteries that FARC supplied ruined countless lives each day.

But when it got down to his *own* pain, Frederico Heredia had no courage at all.

"I used the flat of the blade that time," Bolan finally told the man so he'd quit trying to see if blood was running down his face. To emphasize his words further, he tapped the wide flat side of the knife against his other palm. "But there's no guarantee I won't use the edge if you force me to do it again. So start talking."

"I am with the 14th Front," Heredia said trembling. "Pepe is leader of the 28th. I have no contact with him. I have never met him. I—"

Bolan reached across the man, then brought the wide blade back to smack him across the other cheek in a backhand blow. Another small welt began to rise as the man's entire face turned red. "I don't want to hear about what you *don't* know, Freddie," the Executioner said. "I want you to tell me what you *do* know."

"*Madre de Dios*," Heredia said, tears running down both his reddened and swelling cheeks. "I am a simple member of the 14th Front. Pepe 89 is the leader of the 28th. I swear to you, I know nothing except that he

seems immune from arrest. They—you, perhaps?—
have tried to capture him many times but have failed."

"And why is that so?" Bolan demanded, holding the
bowie up in front of Heredia's eyes once more.

"I do not know," the FARC man said quickly. "I
swear to you…I do not know. Perhaps he has a contact
within the government."

Bolan was tempted to slap him with the flat side of
the blade again but restrained himself. "It doesn't take
a genius to figure that out, Freddie," he said. "Now, you
tell me *who* that contact is, and you might get out of
here alive."

"Ahh," Heredia said, rolling his eyes up into his head
in horror. "I do not know. Please… You must believe me.
I do not know…." His words trailed off and he closed
his eyes tight, certain than his head was about to be
chopped off or his throat cut.

Bolan stood up and walked to the door. Below, he
could see the van. Wilson still sat behind the wheel, but
he had turned sideways in order to keep his eyes on the
man in the back. Behind him, the Executioner could
hear Heredia openly crying. He said again that he knew
nothing more about Pepe 89.

The problem was, the Executioner believed him.

Turning back to the man tied to the chair, Bolan
said, "Okay."

"Okay?" Heredia sniveled. "Okay…what?"

"Okay," Bolan repeated. "I believe you."

A look of shock fell over Heredia's face as he opened
his eyes. "Then you will let me go?" he asked.

"I didn't say that," the Executioner replied. "Not yet,
anyway. You're a low-life scumbag terrorist, Freddie.
Just because you're so worthless at it that they don't

trust you with much information doesn't change that fact. But if you cooperate, there's still a chance you might get out of here and back to Bogotá alive."

Heredia leaned forward against the paracord binding him to the back of the chair. "Tell me what to do!" he almost shouted. "Just tell me what to do! I will do whatever you wish! Anything."

Bolan looked down at the disgusting sight before him. "I want you to pretend you're dead," he said.

Heredia's expression changed to one of amazement. "You want what?"

"I want you to pretend that you're dead," Bolan said. "I'm going to carry you out of here and dump you on the ground near the van. I want the other man in the van to think I killed you." He paused to let it sink in, then went on. "And keep in mind that if he doesn't buy it— doesn't believe you're dead—you soon *will be*. Now, have you got all that straight?"

Heredia began to tremble.

"I will convince him."

"There's one more thing," the Executioner said. So far, there had been no point in asking him about the older man who was still in the van. Heredia had already been unconscious when the man entered the men's room, and was blindfolded by the time they both regained consciousness. But the middle-aged man had known Heredia. And that meant Heredia probably knew him, as well. "You can play dead with your eyes open just as well as with them shut," he said. "I want you to take a good look at the man we're going to bring up here after I dump you on the ground. You know him. And I want you to tell me his name."

"I will tell you if I know him," the FARC man said,

still trembling. "But with my eyes open the whole time? What if I blink and he sees me?"

"Then you'll die," the Executioner said simply. He began digging through Wilson's bags again until he came across one where canned food and other items had been placed. Toward the bottom, he found a bottle of ketchup.

"What is that?" Heredia asked feebly.

"Stage makeup," the Executioner said. Then, setting the bottle on the table, he began to untie Frederico Heredia.

THE SUN HAD FINALLY risen on a new day when Bolan, with Frederico Heredia over his shoulder like a sack of potatoes, walked down the steps to the driver's side of the van. Even through the windshield, he could see the surprised look on Wilson's face. To the former Texas Ranger, it looked as if Bolan really had used the bowie to torture the man to death. And that didn't add up to the man Wilson had grown to know since they'd both arrived in Colombia.

Bolan stared through the windshield, past Wilson, to the rear of the van. The man in the back was still blindfolded.

Bolan quickly shook his head for Wilson's benefit.

The man was sharp. He caught on immediately to what was happening and looked as if he was having trouble not laughing out loud.

Bolan walked up to the driver's window and said, "Take the blindfold off our friend in the back." Then he walked around to the other side of the van.

Wilson exited the driver's seat and hurried after him. A moment later, the door to the rear of the vehicle slid back on its track. Wilson reached in, ripped the shirt off the older man's face, then grabbed him by the shoulders and pulled him out.

Just like Heredia before him, the tough guy fell on his face. Wilson pulled him up to his knees just as Bolan, ten yards or so away from the van, nodded. Then the Executioner leaned forward and dumped Heredia to the ground.

Heredia fell onto his side, his face toward Wilson, the older man, and the van. His eyes were open. And he kept them that way, staring with a thousand-yard gaze as if he was just waiting for rigor mortis to set in.

The older man squinted, trying to let his eyes adjust to the early morning light after being blindfolded for so long. But he saw what he was supposed to see, and took it the way he was supposed to take it. Watching out of the corner of his eye, the Executioner saw his face. For just a second or two, true fear shone in his eyes. But it disappeared just as quickly as it had come, and for a brief moment the man with the scar *smiled*. Then he went back to the solemn demeanor he'd maintained ever since awakening.

That second or two of fear had caught Bolan's attention. On a long-term hard case like this man, it spoke volumes. The smile was hard to explain. The Executioner knew it might mean that the man had forced it onto his face in order to drive out the fear and make his captors believe that nothing could shake him.

On the other hand, it might mean the man suspected the whole thing was a setup.

The hastily hatched plan had flaws, Bolan knew. But even if it failed, one way or another, he was going to know everything both Heredia and the man with the scarred face knew before any of them left the jungle again.

Bolan had brought Heredia's white shirt with him, and he began wiping the "blood" off his own arms with it. Ketchup didn't smell like blood, so he had been careful to drop Heredia downwind of the van, and far enough away that the man Wilson was now jerking to his feet could not pick up the scent. That was the major flaw in his plan—the scent. It meant Bolan had been forced to refrain from spreading more ketchup around the chair in the cottage where Heredia had been seated. He had to count on the drama of what the older man had just witnessed, combined with the grilling the Executioner was about to give him, to keep his mind away from such a trivial detail.

Like so many other aspects of each mission the Executioner took on, the ketchup was a calculated risk that had to be taken.

Wilson had caught on quickly, and he began to write his own lines in the impromptu play. "He dead?" he called across to the Executioner.

"Almost," Bolan said. "And he will be in another minute or so." He paused and looked up at the cottage atop the steps. "Take that maggot on up. I'll be with you in a minute."

"You got it," Wilson said and tugged the older man's arm toward the stairs.

Bolan waited until they had disappeared into the cottage, then leaned down close to Heredia. "You recognize him?" he whispered.

"Hell, yes!" the ketchup-covered man whispered back. "You mean you don't you know who that is?"

"If I did I wouldn't be asking you, would I?" the Executioner said.

"That's Jose Cantu," Heredia said, his eyes wide. "Jose El Toro," they call him sometimes.

"Is he FARC?" Bolan asked.

"No," the man on the ground said. "He's a hit man.

But he knows people in FARC. Probably more than me. They've used him before."

Bolan nodded. He hadn't hit the jackpot, but it looked like he'd at least been dealt a decent hand on which to build. "Well," he said. "Joe the Bull needs to think you're dead. I'm going to fire a shot in the ground next to you. You can flinch when it goes off if you want, but after that you play dead. Move even one muscle and screw things up for me with Cantu, and the next round I fire will be the last you ever hear." He paused. "Actually, they tell me you never hear the one that kills you. But I wouldn't really know about that."

"Wait!" Heredia whispered. "I can't keep my eyes open forever!"

Bolan nodded. He had only needed Heredia to identify the older man. That had been done. "So turn your head away from the house and keep it there after I shoot. If we come down the steps later and you're in any other position, you get one in the head for that, too."

Heredia twisted away from the cottage.

"One more thing," Bolan said. "I know you're thinking about trying to get away. So let me promise you one thing—if I come back out here and you aren't right where you're supposed to be, I'll drop everything else I'm doing, track you down, and kill you *slow*. Get it?"

"Yes," Heredia said.

Bolan stood up straight, drew the Desert Eagle from under his shirt and aimed it a foot to the side of Heredia's face. The man was going to have a hard time hearing out of the ear that wasn't pressed into the ground. But that was a small price to pay for his life.

The Executioner pulled the trigger and the big .44 Magnum pistol exploded. Birds flew from the treetops, monkeys chattered in fright and anger as they swung themselves to new branches, and a variety of ground wildlife scattered, unseen, among the brush.

There was no doubt in Bolan's mind that Jose Cantu would have heard the shot from inside the cottage.

By the time the Executioner had climbed the steps and entered the one-room dwelling again, Wilson had Cantu tied to the same chair where Heredia had sat. The retired Texas Ranger stood a few feet away, cleaning his fingernails with the giant bowie knife. The act, Bolan knew, was designed to subtly intimidate their prisoner even further.

If it was working, it didn't show on Cantu's face. In fact, the middle-aged man even grinned when Bolan walked into the room.

"Smile while you can," the Executioner said, taking the bowie from Wilson. "Because unless you tell us what we want to know, you're going to get the same treatment that your friend Heredia got."

The smile on the killer-for-hire's face widened. "You mean you will slap me around a little, then pour ketchup all over me?" he asked, and laughed out loud.

Bolan nodded. Cantu had either smelled the ketchup in the air in the cottage or when Bolan had walked up to the driver's door to speak with Wilson. Well, that was okay. You won some and you lost some, and some got rained out. But there was always another ball game for those who never gave up, and the Executioner wouldn't have known how to give up if he tried.

Gripping the wooden handle of the large bowie knife, Bolan got ready to swing the flat side against Jose Cantu's face.

"Wait—" the Colombian hit man said. "None of that is necessary."

"You plan to answer my questions, then?" the Executioner asked.

"Of course," Cantu said. "It is you holding the knife...and all of the cards. Besides, I don't know if that little mouse Heredia told you or not, but I am a freelance operative. I owe allegiance only to whoever is paying me. And that allegiance ends when my job is done."

Bolan let the bowie knife fall at his side. "Okay," he said. "I've got a job for you."

"Just tell me who it is," Cantu said. "And he will be dead by tomorrow."

"It's not that kind of job," the Executioner said.

Cantu frowned. "Then what is it you want of me?" he asked.

"I want you to introduce me to the right people," Bolan said. "I want to meet Pepe 89."

Cantu shrugged his shoulders. "It can be done," he said. "But I do have my principles."

Bolan knew what he meant. "How much?" he asked.

"Oh, I should say that thirty thousand of your American dollars would do the trick," he said. "Payable in Colombian pesos, however."

"That can be arranged," the Executioner said. And it could. All he'd need to do was give Stony Man Farm a call and the money could be wired to Colombia through any number of dummy corporations the Farm used for such things.

Bolan looked to Wilson. "Untie him," he said.

The retired Texas Ranger frowned. "You sure?"

The Executioner nodded. "If he tries anything, we'll kill him."

Turning back to Cantu, he added, "And he won't be able to collect any of his thirty large."

"You have a problem," Cantu said as Wilson took the bowie from Bolan and began cutting the paracord that restrained the hit man.

"What problem is that?" Bolan asked.

"That little sissy-shit downstairs in front of the cottage," he said. "I suspect he is still alive?"

"He is," Bolan said. "I kill men when I have to. But I don't murder them." He paused a moment, then said, "Particularly for money."

If the comment offended Cantu, he didn't act like it. "If you let him go, word of what is happening will be all over Bogotá by morning," he said. "Yet I suspect you promised to let him go if he cooperated with you. And I suspect that you have at least one major character flaw."

"What's that?" Bolan asked.

"You strike me as the type of man who does not go back on his word," Cantu said.

"You're both right and wrong," Bolan said. He looked the man in the eye. "I didn't promise to let him go," he said. "I just promised to let him live."

"Ah," Cantu said, standing up and stretching. "You are also a wise man." He stuck his hand in his pants pocket. Bolan waited. He had shaken down both Cantu and Heredia while they were still unconscious and found no weapons on them.

Pulling out his billfold—the same one Bolan had checked in vain for identification—he produced a small white scrap of paper and handed it to the Executioner. "Call this number," he said.

Bolan looked at the paper. A phone number was all that was on it. "Whose is it?" he asked.

"A certain police sergeant in Bogotá with whom I have a…should we say, working relationship?"

For a moment, Bolan wondered if this sergeant might be the leak who warned Pepe 89 each time the police or military were coming. But that wasn't likely. A mere sergeant would be in no position to know everything going on at those levels.

When Bolan said nothing further, Cantu went on. "Call him and tell him you have Heredia handcuffed and waiting. We can dump him somewhere. There are bound to be warrants out on him."

"And if there aren't?" Bolan asked.

"Do not worry," the hit man said. "The sergeant will make sure there are warrants of some kind by the time he picks the man up."

Bolan nodded slowly. He wasn't in favor of framing honest men. But Heredia was hardly an honest man. And if there weren't warrants currently out on him, the Executioner knew there *should* be.

"All right," Bolan said. "We'll find a place to leave Heredia. Since you know him, you make the call." He handed the paper back to Cantu. "And then we'll get to work."

The hit man nodded, then said, "May I have my shirt and jacket back now?"

"After we're on the highway," the Executioner said. "Until then, you're blindfolded again."

"You do not trust me to know where your cabin is?" Cantu asked with mock pain in his voice.

"I don't trust you with *anything*," the Executioner replied.

Cantu shrugged. "We will play the game your way then," he said.

Bolan stared the man in the eyes. "That's *exactly* what we'll do," he said. "But let's get a few things straight right now. I run things. You do exactly what I tell you to do, and the first time you step out of line you'll get a .44 Magnum in your head and the red stuff covering your body won't be ketchup." He paused, took a breath, then continued to stare at the man as he said, "You murder people for money, Cantu. And in my book that makes you no better than Pepe or any of the other FARC trash. I can shoot you or cut your throat, and I'll never lose a moment's sleep." After another pause to let it all sink in, he finished with, "Are we on the same page here?"

"We are," Cantu said cheerfully. "But remember what I told you. Because I meant every last word of it. Until this job is over, I owe all of my allegiance to you. And I will not betray you."

"I hope you'll excuse the both of us if we don't really care to bet our lives on that," Wilson drawled.

Bolan glanced at his partner. He could see tell by looking in Wilson's eyes that the man found the prospect of working with a hired killer like Cantu every bit as distasteful as he did. But both men knew sometimes, there was no other way. Deals with the scum of the earth had to be made on occasions. You didn't infiltrate organizations like FARC with introductions from Sunday-school teachers.

"Let's go," Bolan said. "We'll grab Heredia on the way out and tell him he can quit playing dead."

Without another word, the Executioner turned and led the other men out of the cottage and down the steps.

His hastily put together plan had not worked the way he'd hoped it would.

But with Cantu owing allegiance to no one, and willing to give up anyone on either side of the law if there was enough money involved, it looked like things just might turn out even better.

WILSON DROVE AGAIN, with Bolan in the passenger seat this time. Both of the men in the back had been blindfolded with their shirts, and the ketchup-covered Heredia had begun trembling again. While he hadn't said a word, Bolan knew the man suspected the Executioner was backing out of his agreement and taking him somewhere to kill him.

Bolan waited until they had reached Bogotá's inner city again before directing Wilson through a series of twists and turns. The reason for the roundabout path to nowhere was to throw off Cantu in case he'd been counting time since they'd left the cottage. Some men—Bolan was among them—could do that and, in conjunction with remembering right and left turns, come close to pinpointing the exact location where they'd started even without their eyesight.

Finally, Bolan said, "Turn down this alley.'

Wilson did as he'd been told, then stopped next to a large white trash container when the Executioner pointed to it.

Bolan got out and slid the side door open.

"You are going to kill me!" Heredia screamed.

Bolan looked up and down the alley. There were no listening ears—at least that he could see. "I will if you don't lower your voice," he warned the man.

"Then what *are* you doing?" Heredia asked as Bolan pulled him from the van.

"Leaving you where the police can find you," the Executioner said as he carried the helpless man toward the big white trash receptacle. He had used Wilson's paracord to retie the FARC man's handcuffed wrists to his body behind his back, and more cord to restrain his legs at the ankles. Setting him down next to the trash depository, he lifted the lid.

"But you promised to let me go if I did what you told me to do," Heredia whimpered.

"No," the Executioner said. "I said that if you cooperated there was a chance you'd get back to Bogotá alive. You're now back in Bogotá, you're alive, and that promise has been kept." He lifted Heredia and held him over the foul-smelling garbage inside the bin.

"Where are you putting me!" Heredia screamed.

"Right where men like you belong," the Executioner said. He withdrew his arms, letting the FARC man fall into the trash. The disruption made the container reek even more than it had before. The Executioner closed the lid and walked back to the van.

Wilson had already removed Cantu's shirt, and the man had it halfway buttoned when Bolan pulled his cell phone from his pocket and handed it behind him. "Make your call," he said. "And keep in mind the fact that both of us speak fluent Spanish. If there's even a hint that you're trying to get some other message across to this crooked cop buddy of yours, you'll die before you've even ended the call."

"I would expect no less," Cantu said. "But do not worry. This is exactly the type of thing the sergeant and I do from time to time." He began tapping numbers into the phone. "I feed him arrests such as this that make him look good in the eyes of his superiors. And in turn, he occasionally covers my tracks for me." The Colombian hit man looked up and smiled as the number tried to connect. "Even a professional like myself makes the occasional mistake. When I do, the evidence mysteriously disappears. Just little favors like that."

"Oh yeah," Wilson said sarcastically. "Little favors like covering up murders. Not much different than fixing a speeding ticket."

"Exactly," Cantu said.

A moment later, the Colombian killer made arrangements for Heredia to be picked up.

He hung up, handing the phone back to Bolan.

The van pulled out of the alley as Cantu finished buttoning his shirt. His sport coat had been left in the back of the van ever since Bolan and Wilson had abducted him, and he slipped it on too.

"Where to?" Wilson asked as he began driving.

Bolan looked at the hired killer in the back. He had taken the handcuffs off the man so he could get dressed and make the call. That meant he bore closer watching than ever. You never knew what a man like Cantu might try. On the other hand, the Executioner suspected the promise of his thirty thousand dollars was enough to keep the hit man in line.

At least for the time being.

The Executioner knew that what they needed now was a quiet place where he, Wilson, and Cantu could work out a battle strategy.

The FARCs were no amateurs. If they even suspected that Bolan and Wilson were the law in any form, they'd kill all three men on the spot.

"Find us a hotel somewhere out of the way," Bolan said. "Someplace where we can all sit down and sort things out."

"I know just the place," Cantu said from the back of the van.

"No, thanks," the Executioner replied. "Any place you suggest could very easily be a trap."

He turned to Wilson. "Just keep driving until we see a hotel. I'll check us in."

The Texan nodded, and the van continued on down the street, on its way eventually, Bolan hoped, to Pepe 89.

Or whatever number came after his name by the time they caught up to him.

13

Bolan waited until they were in the second-floor room of the Hotel de Santa Marta before pulling the cell phone from his pocket again. He took a seat on the edge of the bed and tapped the number to Stony Man Farm into the face of the instrument.

While he waited, he looked around the room. Just off Avenue Caracas, the hotel probably wouldn't rate half a star in any tourist guidebook. The two beds were covered with torn and frayed bedspreads, and one of the lamps on the tables to their sides had no shade—just a bare bulb sticking up in the air. As he continued to wait, a cockroach walked confidently past the base of the lamp and disappeared down the other side of the table.

The curtains just beyond a larger table with four chairs were open, and Bolan could barely see through the dirty pane of the sliding glass door. But he could tell the door led to a rusty iron balcony, and offered a view of nothing but the brick side of the building adjacent to the hotel.

Wilson and Cantu had taken seats at the table by the balcony. Both men stared his way while the line connected.

A few seconds later, Barbara Price answered the phone.

Bolan got straight to the point. "I need thirty thousand dollars wired to the Banco de Bogotá," he said. He glanced up and saw Cantu's greedy face grinning. "But I want it in two transactions. Make the first immediately, for ten thousand." He saw Cantu's smile fade at the words. "Don't send the rest until I give you the go."

"I'll get right on it," Price said. "You should have your ten thousand within an hour or so." The Stony Man mission controller asked, "What name do you want it sent to?"

"Jose Cantu," the Executioner said. "He's got an account at the Banco de Bogotá already." He pulled a slip of paper from his pocket on which he'd written the account number Cantu had given him. "Make sure only Cantu can pick it up," Bolan went on. "And set things up so that if he doesn't sign for the ten grand, or the twenty coming later, both wires revert to your end after three days."

"Sounds like you've found yourself a snitch," Price said.

Bolan looked at Cantu, who was pulling an unfiltered cigarette from his shirt pocket. "A *snitch* is exactly what I've found. But I don't trust him as far as I can throw this vermin-infested hotel we're staying in right now. So we need the ten grand just to get his butt moving. If he comes through, I'll give him the other twenty later."

If the words offended Cantu, his face didn't show it.

"You got it, Striker," Price said. "Anything else?"

"Not at the moment."

"Stay in touch."

"I will." Bolan hung up and returned the cell phone to his pocket. Rising, he walked toward one of the two empty chairs at the table.

Wilson sat to his right, his arms folded across his chest.

Cantu had found an ashtray on top of the shoddy room's chest of drawers, and brought it over to the table. Bolan sat down facing the dirt-streaked glass of the sliding door and the bricks of the building a few feet beyond.

"Okay, Jose," Bolan said as he watched the hit man tilt his head back and blow smoke rings through his pursed lips. The perfectly doughnut-shaped little clouds rose, one by one, to the low ceiling before striking it and disintegrating. "Who's your highest connection into Pepe's 28th Front?"

Cantu looked at the Executioner, tapping the ashes off the end of his cigarette into the ashtray. "I have *no* connections to the 28th Front," he said as he smirked.

Bolan leaned forward and backhanded the man across the face just as Cantu stuck the cigarette back into his mouth. He felt the hot embers of the cigarette's tip on the back of his hand for a split second, then both the cigarette and Jose Cantu went flying from the chair. The hired killer landed on his back on the dirty carpet. The chair fell to the side, and the cigarette sailed through the air to fall on the floor next to Wilson.

The Texan reached down calmly and picked the half-crushed butt off the floor, dropping it into the ashtray.

Standing, the Executioner stepped around the corner of the table, reached down and grabbed Cantu by the throat. The man grunted in pain as Bolan hauled him to his feet, then turned the chair upright again and forced him down into it.

"Have I got your attention now, *compadre?*" the Executioner asked.

Cantu's voice came out in a rasp. "Yes," he said.

"We aren't here to play games," Bolan said. "And I don't intend to waste time with you. It goes against my grain to give a scumbag like you one peso, let alone thirty thousand dollars. But I've made a deal with you, and I keep my word. So let's start over. Who's your highest contact to Pepe 89?"

Cantu was rubbing his throat with one hand. His voice was almost a growl when he said, "I was telling you the truth. I have no connections to Pepe 89."

Bolan leaned forward again and brought his arm across his chest for another backhand. But Cantu raised his own hand just in time. "Please!" he whispered. "I was telling you the truth. I have no *direct* contacts into the 28th Front. But I have done jobs for other factions of FARC in the past."

The Executioner settled back in his chair. "Who?" he asked.

"Several," Cantu rasped.

"Start naming them," the Executioner said. "Or you not only miss out on the money, you'll miss out on the rest of your miserable life."

"I killed the mayor of Cartagena for the 14th Front," Cantu grunted. "That was when I met Heredia."

The Executioner remembered the assassination in Cartagena. But it had almost been second page news in Colombia; being the mayor of any city in the country was one of the most dangerous jobs in the world, and several mayors were murdered each year by the FARCs or other terrorist factions. "What part did Heredia play in the Cartagena assassination?" the Executioner asked. He wondered briefly if he might have made the wrong decision in picking Cantu over Heredia as his working informant.

Cantu laughed. With both hands on his Adam's apple, he said, "Heredia did nothing but drive me to and from the city," he said. "He didn't even know my name until we bumped into each other at a night club later. I don't think he ever associated me with the hit in Cartagena, either. Heredia is a peon in the 14th Front. *Estupido*. A nothing."

Bolan nodded, reassured that he'd followed the right hunch in choosing Cantu. "Who did you deal with above Heredia?" he asked.

"A man named Marquez," Cantu said. His voice was coming back a little now but still sounded gravelly. "Ramon Marquez."

The Executioner made a mental note to have Kurtzman gather all of the intel he could on Ramon Marquez. "Does this Marquez know Pepe?" he asked.

Cantu shrugged. "How would I know? He might, and he might not. But my guess is that they would be acquainted."

Bolan nodded slowly. The words rang true. "Do you know anyone else in FARC?" he demanded. "Anyone higher up the food chain than Marquez?"

Cantu shook his head. "I cannot be sure," he said. He stopped speaking to rub his throat again, then went on. "I have taken out three men for the FARCs. All mayors of different cities. And I dealt with different men each time. But I am as ignorant to the inner workings of the organization as you are. The other men with whom I dealt may have been higher in rank, or they may have been lower. I do not know."

"Why do the FARCs need you in the first place?" Bolan asked. "They seem perfectly capable of carrying out their own mayhem without outside help."

"They are," Cantu said. "But the three mayors were popular with the people, and the FARCs didn't want their murders being traced back to them. Politics. FARC still tries to maintain the sympathy of the population— as if their true goal was the welfare of the common man." He paused for a moment, coughed, winced in pain, then went on. "Killing honest *politicos* does not sit well with those common men."

Bolan frowned. "They've killed other mayors and public officials and bragged about it," he said.

"Yes," Cantu nodded. "But those men were known to be dishonest. In those cases it was politically advantageous to be known as their assassins."

Bolan nodded. It made sense. But it also made him dislike, and distrust, Jose Cantu even more. The way it sounded, Cantu had killed *honest* men, which was even worse than taking out public officials who were dirty themselves.

But the Executioner had no time to get into a political debate with the hired killer sitting next to him. "Of the three FARC men you've dealt with," he said, "which one do you know the best?"

"Marquez," Cantu said without hesitation.

"When was the last time you talked to him?"

Cantu squinted slightly, thinking. "A month or so ago. When I picked up the final installment for the Cartagena job."

"Would you have any good reason to contact him now?" the Executioner asked.

"None that I can think of," Cantu said.

Bolan stood. Wilson, who had remained silent during the interrogation, did the same. Cantu, following their leads, stood up, too. "Where are we going?" the hired assassin asked as Bolan turned and walked toward the door to the hall.

The Executioner stopped and turned. "To get your

money at the bank," he said. "It'll give you some time to think."

"Think about what?" Cantu asked.

Bolan grasped the doorknob. "To think of a reason to contact Marquez and introduce me and my friend here into his organization."

"But I told you, I have no reason to contact him again."

"That's why I'm giving you time to think of one." The Executioner opened the door but stood where he was.

"And if I cannot come up with a reason?" Cantu asked. "I do not get to keep even the ten thousand dollars?"

"Not only that," the Executioner said easily. "You don't even get to keep your life."

Bolan saw a flash of fear on the usually stoic hit man's face. Men who had it in them to kill other men recognized each other—even when they were on opposite sides of the law and morality in general. Slightly flustered, Cantu turned to Wilson behind him.

If he was looking for sympathy or support, he had looked in the wrong direction. The retired Texas Ranger reached behind him, pulled out the huge bowie knife, held it up in front of him and tested the razor-sharp edge with his thumb. He smiled.

Jose Cantu realized that while Bolan and Wilson might represent justice rather than the immoral acts he was paid to commit, he was dealing with two men every bit as deadly as himself. Perhaps even more so.

Without another word, the Executioner led them out of the door.

THE PLAN WAS SIMPLE.

But as dangerous as sticking your head into the open mouth of a lion.

Still unnerved by the sudden realization that he was outnumbered by men who would kill him as easily as he would them, Cantu had drawn a mental blank and it had been Bolan who had come up with the basic scenario for the plan of introduction.

Cantu would telephone Ramon Marquez and explain that it was urgent that he meet with him. Bolan and Wilson would accompany the hit man to the meeting and, once they were there, Cantu would explain that he was retiring from the business of hired assassin and moving to parts unknown to live out the rest of his life in peace. He would stress that he had killed too many people in Colombia, could sense that the law was only a step behind him, and was simply getting too old, and too tired, to keep looking over his shoulder all the time.

Cantu would tell Marquez the Americans were both men to whom he had subcontracted in the past; men who had played various roles in several of his hits and in whom he placed one hundred percent trust.

He would explain that they would be available to step into Cantu's shoes and take over, doing any of the dirty work the FARC 14th Front, or any other faction of the terrorist organization, didn't want pinned on them.

As they turned the van into the driveway leading to a locked and guarded gate in one of Bogotá's more affluent northern suburbs, Bolan again saw that the FARC's initial commitment to overthrow the Colombian government in order to benefit the people had been lost somewhere along the way. If it had ever existed at all. The three-story rough rock mansion looked more like a castle than a house.

It was obvious that Ramon Marquez had no plans to live like a "common" Colombian himself.

Cantu was driving, and the guard at the gate recognized him immediately. The hit man's very presence turned the uniformed man's lips down into a solemn expression. It meant something serious was afoot.

"Señor Cantu," the man said as he stepped down from the small guard shack just outside the iron gate. "How are you?"

"I am fine, Mario," Cantu said. "And you?"

"Excellent," the guard replied. He leaned to look inside the van where Bolan and Wilson sat. "Do you have an appointment?" he asked.

"Yes," Cantu said. "Señor Marquez is expecting all three of us."

"I am sorry. But you know the rules," the guard said.

Cantu had already warned Bolan and Wilson that they would be expected to leave their weapons outside the gate, so both men followed the hit man's lead and got out of the van.

Cantu reached into his waistband and produced the Colt Python Wilson had picked up from the AUC man who had driven the van. Bolan had taken all six .357 Magnum rounds out of the weapon and then, with two sets of pliers, pulled out the bullets and dumped the gun powder. Getting the hollowpoint bullets back into the casings had been a little like putting the toothpaste back in the tube, but he had accomplished it without bending the cases so much that they no longer fit into the chambers.

Unless someone actually opened the cylinder and inspected the rounds closely, the Python appeared loaded and ready for action.

As soon as the guard had taken the Colt, Bolan drew his Desert Eagle and Beretta, handing them over along with the TOPS SAW knife. The man's eyes bulged slightly when he saw the big .44 Magnum gun. "You do not fool around, do you?" he said, looking up into Bolan's eyes.

"In our business, fooling around gets you dead," he replied.

Mario nodded as he stuffed all three weapons under the Sam Browne belt he wore. When Wilson drew "Betty" and "Becky" from his sides, Mario said, "*Un momento, por favor*. I have only two hands." Stepping back up into the guard shack, he set the Executioner's weapons somewhere out of sight, then returned to take Wilson's twin .45s. The retired Texas Ranger also pulled out the bowie, along with its sheath, from behind his back and extended it. "You want this too?" he asked.

"*Madre de Dios*," Mario said.

Mario took the .45s and the knife back into the guard shack and pushed a button. The iron gates swung open in front of them as they got back into the van.

Bolan made a mental note about the lax security. The guard had not checked the back of the van, where they had their AK-47s and extra magazines only marginally hidden beneath some of Wilson's equipment bags. Nor had he patted them down after accepting the guns and knives they'd offered.

Bolan still had the little .380 Guardian in his underwear, and Wilson was toting the single action Black Widow in some equally hidden location on his body. Mario either was a bad guard or Jose Cantu was extremely trusted at Ramon Marquez's mansion.

Either way, such knowledge might well come in handy in the future.

With Cantu behind the wheel again, the van pulled slowly through the gate and began winding along the driveway toward the house. As they neared, Bolan said, "You did a good job back there, Cantu. Just make sure you keep it up." He thought about showing the hit man that he was still armed, but hesitated. It might be better that Cantu not know any more than Marquez did.

But a tiny voice in the back of Bolan's head told him to show Cantu the gun anyway. It was the voice of experience, and he had never erred when he followed it.

Bolan pulling the little pistol into view. "Keep in mind that I can still kill you at a moment's notice, Jose," the Executioner said as he showed the tiny gun to the man behind the wheel, then dropped it into the right front pocket of his pants.

Cantu's face fell slightly. But only for a moment.

That moment was enough, however, for Bolan to realize something was up.

Cantu parked the van behind a bright red Hummer in front of the house and the three men got out. Bolan let the hit man lead the way to the door and ring the bell.

A moment later, the door was opened by a man roughly the size of an elephant. Close to seven feet tall and weighing at least four hundred pounds, he was fat. But beneath the fat, the Executioner could tell there was a good deal of muscle, too. He was clean shaved— including his head—and a light film of sweat covered both his face and bald pate.

He was also deaf, the Executioner realized, as Cantu said, "Greetings, Santiago," at the same time signing the words with his hands. "And how are you today?" he continued with both hands and mouth.

The huge man grunted, then he stepped back and waved them in with a hand the size of a canned ham.

Bolan was right behind Cantu, and immediately upon

entering he saw why security at the gate could afford to be so derelict, and why Cantu's face had changed only momentarily when he'd produced the tiny pistol. Directly in front of them in the entryway was a walk-through metal detector—the same type as the ones commonly used at airports. On the other side of the device, the Executioner could see three men.

One of the men was roughly five-ten and 175 pounds. He wore khaki fatigue pants and a green T-shirt. Over the T-shirt was a brown leather shoulder holster holding what looked like a Dan Wesson revolver with a six-inch barrel.

The man's hand was on the big wooden grips as he waited for the guests to pass through the metal detector.

The other two men were dressed similarly. One wore a Government Model .45—which looked plain compared to Betty and Becky—in a cross-draw holster. The third man simply held a Skorpion machine pistol in his hand.

Cantu turned and grinned at the Executioner, and what he had planned suddenly became obvious. So far, the hit man had been both outnumbered and outgunned. But the balance of power had shifted. Compared to the weapons Marquez's men now flaunted, the little .380 auto might as well have been a child's dart gun. And it was about to be found as Bolan walked through the metal detector. The same could be said for Wilson's Black Widow.

Bolan knew he had to act fast. Weapons carry was always a balance between speed and concealability; the more concealed a gun was the slower it was to bring into action. His little .380 was in his pants pocket by necessity, and drawing it would be slow.

Deathly slow. And Wilson's Black Widow—wherever it was—was likely to be just as tardy.

The FARC men had all drawn their weapons and were waiting to shoot all three of Marquez's guests if necessary. And while he didn't bother looking behind him, Bolan suspected the deaf giant had drawn a weapon of some kind as well.

Bolan was fast and accurate. But considering the lopsided odds in both numbers and firepower, he wasn't going to make it out of this gunfight alive. Wilson would try his best to help, Bolan knew. But the retired Texas Ranger would die trying just like the Executioner.

Like so many sudden changes that occurred during his missions, Bolan had to think on his feet. And there was only one course of action he could see that might give them a chance of getting out alive.

Taking advantage of the giant doorman's inability to hear, and the distance still between him and the three men on the other side of the metal detector, Bolan leaned forward quickly and whispered into Cantu's ear, "I suggest you come up with some excuse fast, because you're going to be the first man I shoot before I go down."

Cantu turned, but this time he wasn't smiling.

"Come on," said the man with the big Dan Wesson revolver. "Señor Marquez does not like to be kept waiting."

Cantu walked through the metal detector with no problem. But when the Executioner did the same, he heard the familiar buzz-ring that had become almost like background music at airports around the world.

The man with the Dan Wesson stepped forward, the big revolver aimed at Bolan's gut. "Empty your pockets, then step back through again," he growled.

Bolan did as he'd been ordered, handing his paper money and coins to the man with the Skorpion. The .380

was going to set the metal detector off again, he knew it, and unless he, Wilson, or Cantu came up with something fast a very one-sided gun battle was about to begin.

Bolan stared at Cantu for a moment as he stepped back between the walls of the device. His face said it all: *Do something or you die.*

Cantu—already standing next to the man with the cross-draw holster, said, "Can we not dispense with this bullshit? As you can see, both of my friends are *norteamericanos*, and both suffered wounds in Afghanistan and Iraq. They have *shrapnel* still in their bodies. *That* is what is setting off your little toy."

The Dan Wesson man stared at Cantu, his eyebrows lowering as he tried to decide if the hit man was lying or telling the truth. Finally, he said, "Maybe that's so. I guess we'll just have to strip-search them."

Cantu was proving to be a good actor, as well as a man who could think on his feet and take advantage of whatever openings were served up to him. His face suddenly changing to one of outrage, he shouted, "Strip-search them? You would impose such an indignity on men I bring to this house? After all I have done for Señor Marquez? Never! I will not permit it!" He turned to Bolan and Wilson and said, "Come in. We will take this matter up with Señor Marquez."

Bolan glanced at the faces of the guards and saw the shock Cantu's sudden outburst had caused. For a moment, they stood paralyzed, not knowing what to do. While he had no respect for Jose Cantu, Bolan was becoming more and more certain with each step of the mission that he had been right in choosing this man as his informant. Cantu obviously carried a great deal of weight, at least with the 14th Front of FARC.

"Take us to Senor Marquez *immediately*," Cantu demanded. "Or I will see that you are taken out into the jungle and shot so the jaguars and other animals do not go hungry tonight."

The threat worked. The lead guard said, "Follow me," and the others turned their backs to Bolan, Wilson and Cantu.

The Executioner looked over his shoulder as he followed the men through the metal detector, setting it off again. The device buzzed when Wilson walked through, then a final time as the deaf man crossed between the electronic eyes. Bolan saw that the man had drawn a gun, and it was one that fit his size.

Bolan was staring down the hole of a stainless-steel S&W .500 Magnum revolver. As he began to turn back, the bald hulk opened his sport coat and dropped the revolver back into a hip holster.

The three guards led the way to a large office, with a huge oak desk covered with papers and other paraphernalia in the center of the room. File cabinets, computer hutches, two couches, and a variety of other chairs and tables filled the rest of the room.

A man in his late forties or early fifties sat behind the desk. He wore a full beard that had once been black but was streaked with gray, green army fatigue pants and blouse, and a matching cap. In his mouth was a large Churchill cigar.

It didn't take much imagination to figure out who the man had styled himself after. Or who had provided the cigar, and probably the funding for the FARCs in their early days of revolution.

The Fidel Castro copycat stood behind the desk. "Greetings, Jose," he said. He glanced at his men. "It sounded as if I heard arguing downstairs. Was there some problem?"

"Yes, Senor Marquez," Cantu said, sounding irritated. "These men practically accused my friends of wanting to assassinate you. Both have shrapnel from wounds they suffered in the Middle East, and that shrapnel set off the metal detectors. So your men wanted to subject them to a strip search. I would not allow such an affront to take place with men for whom I hold such high regard."

Marquez smiled. "My men were only doing as I had ordered them to do, Jose," he said in a pleasant voice.

"Señor Marquez," Cantu went on, "I understand your need for security. And I am willing to humble myself to a certain degree because of that need. But this went too far. It would have been humiliating to my two friends—both of whom are important men I want you to meet. And it was insulting to me. After all of the times I have worked for you, I believe I am entitled to a little more respect than these cretins have shown us." He stood tall, chin out, waiting for an answer.

Bolan waited, too. He knew Cantu was gambling at this point, and perhaps even overplaying his hand. Calling Marquez's men *cretins* was an indirect insult to Marquez himself.

For a moment, Marquez didn't respond. Then, obviously choosing to ignore the roundabout disrespect, he leaned forward and opened the lid to a large humidor. Pulling out three Cuban cigars like the one already in his mouth, he handed one each to Cantu, Bolan and Wilson. All three men accepted the peace offering as a signal that the house guards' mistreatment had been evened out by Cantu's own discourtesy, and the scoreboard was now even.

Looking at his men as he handed out the cigars, the FARC leader dismissed them, "Go back downstairs. Everything is fine," he assured them.

The men with the guns disappeared out the door.

Marquez motioned for his guests to sit down, and Bolan and Wilson took seats on a couch directly in front of the desk. Cantu chose an overstuffed armchair just to the side. The 14th Front leader opened a desk drawer and pulled out a gold lighter, handing it across the desk to Cantu before resuming his own seat.

The three visitors took turns lighting their cigars.

When all three men were clouding the room with grayish smoke, Marquez spoke again. "So, Jose," he said, "tell my why this meeting with these men is so urgent, if you will?"

But before the hit man could answer, Marquez glanced at Wilson's Texas Ranger hat, looked away, then did a double take. Holding up a hand to stop Cantu's answer, he said, "What an interesting hatband you have."

Wilson proved once again that he was up to any unexpected event that came up undercover. "Thank you, Señor Marquez," he said. "I like it myself." He grinned. "You might call it a gift. Of sorts."

"Am I to understand that a Texas Ranger gave you the hat?" Marquez asked.

"Not exactly," Wilson said. "As best I can remember it, he was a little reluctant to part with it." His smile widened. "He seemed to feel the same way when I relieved him of his guns and badge." Drawing deep on his cigar, he let the smoke trail out of his mouth as he finished. "Of course by that time, the man really had no use for them anymore."

Marquez read between the lines, and laughed. "We all like our trophies, I suppose," he said.

Finally turning his attention back to Cantu, he said, "Forgive the interruption, Jose, but it is not every day that a man wearing the hat of a Texas Ranger walks into my office. Please. Go on."

"I'm retiring," Cantu said bluntly. "I've got too much heat on me, I'm getting too old, and I'm sick of peeking through the curtains and getting sick to my stomach every time my doorbell rings."

"But you are so good at what you do, my friend. In fact you are the best."

"Not anymore," Cantu said. "I'm tired, and maybe no one else sees it yet but I can feel myself slipping."

"That is a shame," Marquez said. "Can you tell me where you will be going in your retirement?"

"With all due respect, Ramon," Cantu said, "I'd rather not." He paused to draw on his cigar, then went on. "I feel like it would be best if I disappeared from this whole side of the world. I've killed men from Argentina to Northern Canada, and if I don't get out of here soon one of those jobs is going to catch up to me. I can't exactly explain it, Ramon. But I know that my time is running out. I can feel *it* right here." He tapped his chest with a fist. "Do you understand what I mean?"

Bolan and Wilson sat passively as the two men spoke as if they were not even in the room.

"*Sí, mi amigo*," Marquez said, nodding. "Such feelings are abstract and hard to explain. But I understand these premonitions better than most men. That is why I am still alive while others are dead." His cigar had burned down almost to the end, and he removed it from his teeth as he went on. "I applaud your good sense in knowing when the time to quit has arrived." Giving up on the stub of Cuban tobacco in his hand, he dropped it into a large ceramic ashtray on his desk. "But I must tell you this. As I said, you are the best at what you do. And you will be sorely missed. I do not know how I will replace you."

"I appreciate such kind words," Cantu said. "But I would never leave you empty-handed. I know there will be more jobs in the future to which you do not want to be linked. That is why I have brought these two men to meet you."

Marquez turned to stare at Bolan and Wilson. Both men were puffing away on their cigars. "Have you worked with them in the past, Jose?" he asked without looking back at the hit man.

"Oh yes," Cantu said. "I have used them in various roles, on many occasions, and in several countries. And both have even been my triggermen a time or two. I have complete trust in both their loyalty and abilities."

Marquez stared at Bolan and Wilson for a moment, then looked back to Cantu. When he did, his face had changed slightly. "My only concern, Jose," he said, "is that the timing on all of this is very strange. Perhaps you are not aware of it, but I received word several days ago that two very special American agents were entering Colombia. They would be undercover, and coming after our organization—one man in particular. My friend, Pepe, who I understand now carries the numeral 89 after his name instead of 88."

Cantu put a puzzled look on his face. "No, I was not aware of that. But—"

Marquez held up his hand to stop the man's answer.

Bolan sat quietly, waiting. Both he and Wilson knew that word of their entry into the country had to have come to Marquez from Pepe 89, who had received it from whoever his government source was. But in these roles they were playing as Cantu's sidekicks, they would not know that. So both men looked curiously back as well.

"Surely you heard about the gunfight at the airport a few days ago," Marquez said, addressing Cantu once more.

"Yes, of course," the hit man replied.

"Are you certain it was not these two Americans, old friend? And that they are not, in some way, now forcing you to introduce them to me as friends?"

For a moment, silence ruled the room. Then, in a voice of false shock, Cantu said, "Ramon! I am dismayed that you would even consider the possibility that I would betray you in such a manner."

Marquez nodded slowly, looking back and forth over the three men in front of his desk. "I do not believe you would do so willingly," he finally told Cantu. "Because our working relationship has always been financially advantageous to you. In fact, I like to believe that much of the money that I have paid you over the years contributes to the fact that you are now in a position to retire to whatever remote part of the world you intend to go." He continued to stare into the hit man's eyes. "But sometimes even the most loyal of men find themselves suddenly thrown into positions of disadvantage that require them to do things they never dreamed they would do to insure their own survival." His stare intensified as he finished his speech, "Could this be one of those time, Jose?"

"Certainly not," Cantu said quickly and firmly. He took a drag off his cigar, then spoke in the same confident voice. "Correct me if I am wrong, Ramon, but from what I heard about the gunfight at the airport, one of the agents had blond hair and a beard. As you can see, neither of my friends here—my *old and trusted* friends—match that description."

Marquez nodded. "No," he said. "Obviously, they do not. But disguises are not out of the question, either. Hair can be dyed. Beards can be shaved." He opened the humidor, pulled out another cigar and clipped the end with a tiny silver cigar cutter. "They were also described as both being large men—one larger than the other. Your friends *do* fit that part of description. That would be impossible to change." Sticking the new cigar between his teeth, he used the gold lighter to light it as he twirled the end around with his other hand.

Bolan decided it was time to step in. Looking to Cantu, he said simply, "Let's go, Jose. This man doesn't trust us, and I can't really say I blame him under the circumstances. Too much coincidence. Perhaps sometime in the future things will be different. But in the meantime, we have plenty of other work to keep us busy." He stood up and Wilson rose next to him.

The FARC leader reached out, motioning Bolan and Wilson to resume their seats. "*Por favor*," he said. "Let us not dismiss this potentially mutually advantageous working relationship quite so abruptly. Perhaps we can work something out which is agreeable to us both."

Bolan and Wilson glanced at each other, then sat back down.

"I neither trust nor distrust you at this point," Marquez said. "I simply do not know. And while you may, indeed, have plenty of other work—Colombia has many people who need to be killed—I doubt that this work will pay you as well as I am able to do."

Cantu was still playing his part well. He shrugged,

looked at the Americans, and said, "It is true. Señor Marquez has always been a very generous employer."

"All I ask," Marquez said, "is that you do something to prove to me that you are not the American agents about whom I have been warned. Or some other kind of law-enforcement officers who are my enemies rather than my friends."

Wilson spoke for the first time since the discussion about his hat. "I'm sure we can do that," he drawled. "As long as this *something* pays well, too."

Bolan nodded in agreement.

Marquez laughed. "I would not expect you to work free, even during this trial period," he said. "So I will give you a small test of loyalty—a simple job through which you can prove to me that you are to be trusted in the future." Whirling on the wheels of his desk chair, he leaned down and opened the bottom drawer of a gray file cabinet directly behind him. What he was doing was out of the sight of the men seated in front of the desk, but they could hear the shuffle of papers. After several moments, Marquez turned around holding a light brown file and dropped it on the desk in front of him, turning it to face away from him.

Bolan, Wilson and Cantu all leaned forward.

When Marquez opened the file, they saw the stern face of a mustachioed man wearing the uniform of the Colombian National Police staring back at them. He stood outside of what looked like some sort of municipal building, and the photo appeared to have been taken with a long-range lens.

"This is Captain Pedro Guttierez," said the man behind the desk. "He is what you Americans call a real..." He paused for a moment, searching for the right words, then said, "Pain in the arse?"

"It's the Brits who say 'arse,'" Wilson said with a laugh. "We just say ass. But we get your drift."

"He is a fool, no matter what else we call him," Marquez said. "I have offered to make him a millionaire many times. He has always refused." He took a slow drag on his cigar, then let the smoke out as he continued to speak. "It seems that he is incorruptible."

"So you'd like him dead, I take it," Bolan said, reaching out and lifting the picture out of the file for closer inspection.

"*Sí,*" Marquez replied. "I would very much like him dead. And I will pay you twenty-five thousand dollars each to do me this favor. A favor which, I do not believe, any American agent would do."

The Executioner nodded. "Consider him dead," he said, and stood up. Leaning over the desk, he dropped the picture back into the file and closed it. Then lifting the entire file in his hand, he said, "We can take this with us?"

"Of course," Marquez said.

All four men rose to their feet now and handshakes were exchanged around the desk. "How long will it take you?" Marquez asked.

"I don't know," Bolan said. "It depends on Guttierez's schedule. A day. Maybe two."

"I will, of course, require absolute proof that he is dead," said the leader of the FARC 14th Front.

"What is it you want?" Bolan asked. "I can take pictures. And bring you some of Guttierez's personal items. The captain's bars from his uniform. The whole uniform if you want it. Things like that." He glanced down at the file in his hands. "In the picture, it looked like he was wearing some kind of Colombian National Police signet ring. You want us to bring you that?"

"No," Marquez said. "I'm afraid none of those things will do. I am familiar with how undercover operatives sometimes fake murders, and all of the items you mentioned are far too easy to forge. You must remember—this assignment is your proving ground, and I must be absolutely certain that the captain is dead." The leader of the FARC 14th Front paused for a moment, frowning into space, thinking. Then, slowly, his lips curled up into a deadly grimace.

"Bring me Guttierez's head," Marquez told the Executioner. "Yes. The head. The head will do fine. It will be easier than transporting the entire body, and I will recognize his face."

It was Bolan's turn to pause. "That could present a problem," he said. "I like to work a little differently than Cantu." He glanced at the hit man, who took the cue like an award winning actor.

"My trusted friend, Señor Cooper, favors the 12-gauge shotgun at close range," Cantu said. "It is fast and sure. But afterward…well, as you might imagine, one cannot always recognize the face."

Marquez looked at all three of the men across the desk with suspicion. "That sounds very much like something men who planned to present me with a false head might say," he told them. The broad smile that had covered his face only a moment earlier was reduced to only the corners of his mouth. "In fact, it sounds exactly like something American agents—who had something they were holding over the head of a Colombian killer-for-hire—might try in order to trick me."

The Executioner nodded. "Yeah, I can see how it might sound that way," he said. "But what Jose just told you happens to be the truth." He stopped talking, drew in a breath, then said, "We all have our own personal styles. But I tell you what—I'll do my best to kill Guttierez in a way that doesn't make too much of a mess out of his face. On the other hand, you know how these things go. You never know for sure what'll really happen. Killing a CNP captain isn't going to be the easiest hit in the world, which means I might just have to pull it off within my own personal comfort zone." He paused so his words could sink in with the FARC leader. "So, just in case things come down in a way that I have to blow him away with double-aught buckshot, and all that's left of his face is mush, give me some alternate plan. Is there any other kind of proof that'll suit you?"

Marquez stared into Bolan's eyes, trying to look into his soul and discern if the man was telling him the truth.

Bolan saw in Marquez's eyes that he wasn't sure what to believe.

"If the face is not recognizable," the FARC leader finally said, "you will have to bring the whole body. No, wait. Bring me his hands. Yes, the hands will do fine. Cut off his hands and bring them to me."

Bolan knew instantly what that meant. Through some contact—probably another dirty Colombian cop who was being paid off—Marquez had access to the Colombian National Police fingerprint files. And as a member of that nation-wide police force, Guttierez's prints would be in his personnel records.

If Marquez had the man's hands, he could have one of his men roll the prints and then compare them to those on record with the CNP.

"Consider it a done deal," Bolan said. "You'll either get the head or hands." Then, turning first to Wilson and then Cantu, he said, "Ready?"

Both men nodded.

The Executioner led the way out of the office, his mind racing with what lay ahead of him. FARC 14th Front leader Ramon Marquez—who had already mentioned Pepe 89 and appeared to be a direct link to their target if Bolan and Wilson could pass this initiation test, wanted an honest and incorruptible Colombian National Police captain dead, and the man's head or hands served up on a silver platter.

Things weren't going to be simple.

The Executioner had to figure out a way to kill a man without really killing him.

14

"I need you to hack into the Colombian National Police personnel files, Bear," Bolan said into the cell phone. He sat in the shotgun seat of the white van. In his peripheral vision he could see Wilson turned sideways in the driver's seat.

After Cantu's little trick of not warning them about the metal detector at Marquez's house, neither the retired Texas Ranger nor Bolan was sure that the promise of $30,000 was sufficient to keep the man from turning on them. Cantu would merit a close watch, and Wilson had taken over the "babysitting" chores while Bolan made his call.

"Then what?" Kurtzman asked on the other end of the scrambled and secure line.

"I'll be faxing you a set of fingerprints from a dead man. He was AUC—so my guess is he's got an arrest record, which means his prints will be on file, too." The Executioner paused to take a quick breath. "Then I'll need you to switch the Henry System print classifications so that Captain Guttierez's classification goes into the dead AUC man's file, and the dead man's prints show up as Guttierez's."

"What if there's no record of the AUC guy's to switch?" Kurtzman asked.

"Then we're in trouble," the Executioner said. "And I'll have to think of something else. But I've got several pairs of dead hands we can try. And I'd say it's about a million to one chance that *none* of them have ever been arrested and inked."

"Affirmative," Kurtzman said. "I'll get on it.'

Bolan ended the call and sat back. It was his turn to twist in his seat to watch Cantu as Wilson drove them north, toward the salt mines, and the dead terrorists they had left there. As he kept one eye on the hit man behind him, the Executioner's thoughts turned to the unpleasant task ahead.

Either he, or Wilson, was going to have to sever the hands of one of the AUC men he'd carried into the salt mine the night before so they could take them to Marquez. He could see no way around it. And another less grizzly but even more problematic obstacle lay before them as well.

Bodies wouldn't decay as quickly in conditions such as those around the deserted salt mine as they did in the hotter weather. But the fact that the Executioner had pulled the dead terrorists out of the sun and into the cave would have slowed that deterioration process some— but not completely.

Bolan wondered just how well versed Marquez and his men—for he would surely assign the appalling task of rolling the prints from the severed hands to someone else—might be in the decomposition of dead bodies. Could the of FARC members tell the difference between hands that had been dead for a day compared to those that were only a few hours old?

Bolan didn't know. But he knew that before the day was over he would have found out.

As they neared the northern outskirts of Bogotá, the Executioner spotted a modern supermarket. "Pull in there," he told Wilson.

The retired Texas Ranger did as instructed.

"Watch our buddy until I get back," Bolan said as he got out of the vehicle, and walked into the store.

A few minutes later he had returned with a cooler in his arms. Hidden under the lid was a bag of ice, a squeeze bottle of waterless hand cleaner, and a sheath of white typing paper. He slid the van's side door open and set the cooler in the back next to where Cantu sat cross-legged on the floor. Before he could close the door again, he saw Wilson shiver in mock horror in the driver's seat.

"*This* is sure gonna be fun," the retired Ranger said as the Executioner returned to his seat in the front.

The former AUC van continued north on the four-lane divided thoroughfare, stopping at traffic lights every mile or so and waiting until they turned green. They were in the right-hand lane, halted at the last light before the divided highway turned into the more narrow two-lane road toward the abandoned salt mines, when the Executioner saw Wilson turn his head toward the vehicle stopped next to them.

"Uh-oh," Wilson said.

"What's the problem?" Bolan asked. From where he sat, he could not see the lower-riding vehicle next to the van.

Wilson turned his eyes back to the front but reached up, twisting the rearview mirror sideways so he could continue watching whatever it was that had caught his eye. "We got a hard case riding shotgun in a black four-door Plymouth next to us," he said out of the side of his mouth. "And he's really giving me the eye." He stopped speaking for a moment, then went on. "Now he's looking the van over good." After another short pause, "And now he's turned around, saying something to the driver. My guess is he's telling the man about the bullet holes. Whatever it is, everybody in the car has started chattering like a whole herd of monkeys."

The red light holding them in place turned green and Wilson pulled through the intersection. Bolan twisted in his seat so he could see out of the tinted windows in the van's rear doors.

A black bearded face drove the Plymouth. The man Wilson had spoken of in the passenger's seat wore a huge Zapata-style mustache. It was impossible to tell there were more men in the vehicle's back seat. "They've changed lanes," the Executioner told Wilson. "They're behind us now. Could you tell if there were more men in the back?"

"Yeah," the retired Texas Ranger drawled as he returned the rearview mirror to its original position. "At least two."

Cantu had turned around to stare out of the van's darkened rear windows as well. "You recognize either of those faces?" Bolan asked the hit man.

Jose Cantu shook his head. "No," he said. "But my guess is that they are AUC."

Bolan nodded. That was his guess, too. It had been more than a day since he and Wilson had allowed themselves to be abducted by the right-wing terrorists, and it only made sense that other members of that organization would be wondering what had happened to the van, and the men the Executioner had dragged into the mine.

They were being followed—probably by AUC men who were on their way to check out the same abandoned salt mine toward which they themselves were headed.

Wilson was dividing his attention between the road ahead and the rearview mirror. "They're checking the tag," he said out loud as much to himself as Bolan or Cantu. "Now they're *sure* that this is their van. And when you add that to the fact that their men are missing, there's an unknown gringo face driving this thing, and it's got several brand-new bullet holes in the side, I'd say it's a fair guess they've come to the conclusion that something's wrong." His words came out in the mildly sarcastic tone to which the Executioner had grown accustomed.

Bolan knew he couldn't have summed their current situation up any better himself.

"So what do I do?" Wilson asked the Executioner when the men remained silent.

"Just keep driving for now," Bolan said. Reaching under his arm, he drew the Beretta 93-R from under his unbuttoned shirt. "Cantu," he said, aiming the long sound suppressor into the back of the van at the man's head, "under those gear bags you'll find a pair of AK-47s. I want you to hand them up front to me. *Very carefully*. Stocks first. If either of the barrels even looks like it might start pointing our way, you'll get a 9 mm right through that evil brain of yours."

Cantu moved the bags to the side and cursed under his breath. Bolan could tell he was angry at himself for not finding the assault rifles earlier. On the other hand, he had never had the chance. He had either been bound and blindfolded, or been under the watchful eyes of Bolan or Wilson or both, every time he'd ridden in the van.

When both AK-47s were in the front of the vehicle, the Executioner jammed the Beretta back into his shoulder rig and checked the magazines, then pulled back the bolts and chambered the first rounds. Reaching forward of the receiver, he flipped the safeties on, then dropped the rifle barrels to the floor next to his feet. The stocks now rested on the seat just to his left, where both he and Wilson could reach them at a moment's notice.

In addition to the Soviet-made rifles, Wilson's sawed-off 12-gauge was under the front seat behind his legs.

The van slowed as the highway narrowed to two lanes, then continued on toward the salt mine. The Plymouth followed, with several other cars trailing behind. Now and then, the Executioner caught a glimpse of other heads in the back seat of the Plymouth when they rounded a curve or started up an incline. As Wilson had said, there were at least two more men in the back seat of the AUC car following them. And there could have been three. So the car might contain up to five AUC terrorists. All of whom would be heavily armed.

Wilson had continued to follow the drama in the rearview mirror. "When do you think they'll make their move?" he asked.

"Probably just as we turn off the highway onto the road leading to the mine," the Executioner said.

"How do you know that?" Cantu asked.

"Because that's when I'd do it," Bolan said. "Until then, they think they can pass themselves off as just more traffic going down the same road we're going down. But when we turn off, and they follow, they'll know we know something's up."

The hit man in the back of the van moved closer to

the front. "Give me one of the rifles," he said. "I can take
out the whole vehicle through the rear windows."

For a moment, Bolan considered it. As evil as he
might be, Cantu was still an experienced gunman. And
he could hold the Beretta on the back of the man's head
while he shot, insuring that the man didn't try to turn the
weapon on him and Wilson. Better yet, he could climb
over the seat and shoot through the windows himself.
But as he considered these possibilities, a flash of black
and white caught the corner of his eye to the side of the
van. Turning his eyes for a moment, he saw a Colombian National Police car parked at the side of the road.
A radar gun extended through the driver's open window.

The Executioner discarded the back window plan on
the spot. Even if he waited until they were out of earshot of the CNP vehicle to start firing, there was a better than even chance that there were more of Colombia's
national cops in the area. Traffic control was pretty
much run the same the world over, and police officers
knew that speeding motorists slowed as soon as they
saw a marked unit. They stayed below the speed limit
until that marked vehicle was out of sight, then sped up
again, congratulating themselves on outwitting the trap.

That was when the second car took over and caught
them.

Bolan already had a carload of right-wing terrorists
to worry about. Further complications with the Colombian National Police were the last thing he needed
at the moment.

Cantu's ever-watchful eyes had spotted the traffic
control vehicle, too. He understood immediately when
the Executioner finally answered with, "Bad idea."

"At least give me a gun," the hit man said, turning his

eyes to the front of the van. "We're going to have to fight them sooner or later. I can help."

"You've already got a gun," Wilson said, grinning from behind the wheel. "The Colt Python."

"A gun that *works*!" Cantu half shouted from behind him.

"Oh, you want *that kind* of gun," the retired Texas Ranger said innocently. "Sorry. No can do, amigo."

The hit man looked to Bolan for support. The only reply he got was a shake of the Executioner's head.

The van continued down the two-lane highway, staying just under the speed limit. Less than a mile before they came to the road to the salt mine, they passed a second CNP vehicle, radar gun extended from the window, just like the first.

Bolan frowned. He had planned to instruct Wilson to skid the van into a U-turn almost as soon as they left the highway. Then, he and the retired Texas Ranger would simply lean out their doors and riddle the Plymouth with 7.62 mm rounds. But with a CNP car so close to the turn-off, he couldn't chance the fact that they might hear the gunshots.

They would have to continue on toward the salt mine before the battle began.

"They saw the police cars as well as we did," Cantu said, as if reading the Executioner's mind. "And they will not hesitate to kill any responding officers like you two would."

Bolan nodded. One of the only advantages they'd have had in the battle was to start it before the AUC men trailing them were ready. And that advantage was gone. Squinting again, he thought hard, doing his best to remember the twists and turns in the road from the mine

to the highway. He and Wilson had been on the floor of
the van, with no good view of the pathway, when the
kidnappers had taken them down the road the night before. And it had still been dark when he and the retired
Texas Ranger drove back to the highway after killing the
terrorists. Besides that, the Executioner had not expected to be returning to the mine, and had let his mind
concentrate on furthering his plan of attack toward Pepe
89 rather than memorizing the terrain.

The road leading off the highway appeared in the distance. Wilson began to slow the van. "What d'ya have
in mind, Chief?" the former blacksuit asked calmly.

"They'll know for sure we've spotted them as soon
as they follow us off the pavement," the Executioner
said. "So hit the gas as soon as the tires touch the gravel.
Get as much lead on them as you can, then skid us to a
halt right after the first twist we take that's curved
enough to get us out of their sight for a second or so."

"Sounds good to me," Wilson said as he twisted the
wheel to the left, leaving the highway. "Or at least as
good as things are likely to get, under the circumstances."

"It sounds like a good way to get killed," Cantu said
from the rear of the van. "If I were you, I'd just stay on
the highway."

"Well," Bolan said as he watched the Plymouth slow
and begin to turn behind them, "you aren't us."

"A blessing I'll remember to thank God for tonight,
come bedtime," added the retired Texas Ranger. As soon
as the words had left his mouth, he floored the gas pedal
and the van shot forward. The rear tires kicked up a
spray of dry dirt and gravel, and for a few moments the
Plymouth disappeared behind the brown cloud.

Then, as the dust behind them began to settle, Bolan

saw the car again. Wilson's sudden burst of speed had gotten them roughly thirty yards ahead. But that wouldn't give them much time to stop the van, grab their rifles and get ready before the AUC terrorists were on their tail.

Besides, Bolan saw as the brown cloud behind them finally settled back to the ground, the Plymouth, packed with armed AUC terrorists intent on killing them, had sped up, too.

And extending out of both the front and rear windows of the vehicle, the Executioner could see rifle barrels.

15

There were several red telephones scattered throughout Carlos Gomez-Garcia's ranch house on the side of the mountain facing the jungle, but no one was allowed to answer them but him. Jaime and Antonio—and formerly his old friend Julio—had taken care of business on the other lines leading into the house.

Pepe 89's red phones rarely rang. But when they did, they could mean only one thing.

He picked up the receiver in his study just after the first ring.

"They are coming," the voice on the other end of the call said.

"Police or military?" Gomez-Garcia asked.

"Military," the voice said. "Junglas."

"Ah." Pepe 89 laughed. "The Junglas. Well, they have come before. They will go away just as empty-handed as always." He paused, then asked casually, "I will need to instruct Juan what to do in my absence. How long do I have? When did they leave?"

"The helicopters just took off," the mysterious voice said. "You have at least an hour."

"Yes, perhaps I should take a shower first," the leader of FARC's 28th Front joked.

"You should take these things more seriously," the voice said. "Do not leave anything behind you that would allow them to seize the house and ranch."

"Thank you, my friend," Pepe said sarcastically. "That is something I had never thought of."

"And my money?" the voice asked.

"Will be deposited in your account tomorrow, as always. Is there anything else I should know?"

"No," the voice said and hung up.

Gomez-Garcia looked at the red receiver in his hand for a moment, then replaced it in its cradle. He had joked about taking a shower. But he *did have* at least an hour before the Black Hawk helicopters even appeared in the sky.

Which meant there was time for something else. And it would serve as a fine goodbye.

He left the study and walked casually up the steps to the second floor of the mansion. He found Michelle taking a nap in his bedroom. As usual, the woman was naked.

He took his own clothes off and dropped them on the floor before lying down next to her. Slowly, gently, he caressed her face until she opened her eyes.

The only way to describe their lovemaking, Pepe 89 thought when they were right in the middle of it, was like two jungle jaguars in heat.

When they were finished, Gomez-Garcia lifted his wristwatch from the table next to the bed and said, "We must get up."

Michelle smiled provocatively. "No," she said. "Only *you* must get up again." She started to lean her head down over him. "I will help you."

He grabbed the woman by the shoulders and pulled her head back up to his. "No," he said. "I am serious. The Junglas are on their way."

"What are Junglas?"

The FARC leader was already out of bed and on his feet, slipping his shirt over his head. "A special section of the military," he said. "Like your American Green Berets. They come to arrest me every so often, and my staff and I must leave until they are gone."

The woman rose to her knees on the bed. "It sounds exciting," she purred. "May I come with you?"

He turned to look at her. Michelle's body was perfect, and he regretted that he really did have no more time to spend with her on the bed. "I would have it no other way, my darling," he said as he stooped to pick up his slacks.

A few minutes later, Pepe 89 walked to the wall next to the bedroom door and flipped what appeared to be an ordinary light switch. But instead of adding to the illumination of the room, a loud, wailing alarm began to sound throughout the house. Speakers attached to fence posts, barns and other outbuildings would send the signal to every corner of his ranch, and he knew that within a few minutes all of the men with outstanding arrest warrants would meet him and Michelle in the hidden portion of the mansion's basement. The ranch hands and house servants—who he made sure stayed out of the 28th Front's kidnappings, drug trafficking and other crimes—would be the only ones left to greet the Junglas when they arrived.

Holding the door for Michelle, Gomez-Garcia ushered her into the hall, then down the steps to the first floor. In the pantry just off the kitchen, he reached up to one of the shelves and removed a gallon can of pinto beans.

As soon as the beans had risen into the air, the wall holding the canned vegetables, fruits and other foods began to swivel to the left, revealing a dark passage behind the wall.

A light came on and the wall behind them swung shut again. He led Michelle down a steep rock incline to a small ten-by-twelve-foot room where Jaime and Antonio were already waiting. "Does anyone else need to come with us?" Gomez-Garcia asked his men.

"No," Jaime said, shaking his head. "The rest are either already on the boat or somewhere else, attending to…" He stopped speaking for a moment, looked at Michelle, then finished simply with, "Attending to business."

"Then let us proceed," Gomez-Garcia said. Reaching up to the rock wall, he pulled out a stone the size of his fist. A second later, the sound of steel grinding against rock sounded throughout the room as the counterweights built into the wall went to work. A hidden door of stone slid open with just enough space to allow them to enter, one by one.

Jaime and Antonio stepped back and motioned for the woman to go first. When he saw the fear on Michelle's face, the FARC leader said, "Do not worry, my sweet. The lights on the other side should have come on at the same time as these."

Michelle moved cautiously through the crack in the wall. She was followed by Antonio and Jaime, with Gomez-Garcia bringing up the rear. By the time he entered the long mountain tunnel, the fear had disappeared from the blond beauty's face.

Gomez-Garcia took the woman's arm as they followed Antonio and Jaime through the tunnel. The rock walls on both sides shone with condensation in the dimly lit overhead bulbs. And their footsteps echoed hollowly down the long corridor. They had walked for almost five minutes, twisting and turning—sometimes at a steep downhill grade, other times almost flat—before a brighter light appeared at the end of the tunnel.

Through the exit, they could see the green of the jungle.

Michelle had no fear at all about being the first out of the tunnel and into the light, and she clapped her hands in delight when she saw the water through the trees. "It is a hidden inlet just off the Rio Cusiana," Gomez-Garcia said as he stepped behind her and wrapped his arms affectionately around her waist. "It leads down out of the mountains, then feeds into the Meta which leads all the way to Venezuela should we need to go that far. But I am sure we will not—we never do." Removing one hand, he pointed through a hole in the leaves where part of the shining white bow of a boat could be seen. "My yacht will get us safely away from those nasty old Junglas," he said. Then he kissed her lovingly on the back of the neck.

By the time they had maneuvered through the trees to the dock, Gomez-Garcia could see several of his drug mules, wanted by both police and military, already on board the forty-foot motor yacht. They had left the ladder to the main deck down, and were only waiting on the late-comers before pulling away.

Gomez-Garcia led Michelle up the steps to the deck with Antonio and Jaime following. The captain of the yacht, wearing a crisp khaki shirt, matching pants and a skipper's cap with an anchor crest on the brim, stepped forward. "Is there anyone else coming?" he asked.

Gomez-Garcia shook his head. Slowly, he turned a full 360 degrees on the deck, halting briefly each time he saw the mirror signal of the three snipers strategically placed in the mountains surrounding the river inlet. He had well-trained men guarding the yacht twenty-four hours a day in case government officials—or anyone else—stumbled upon the craft's hiding place. So far, the police and military were both completely ignorant of the spot. But several hikers and the operator of one small sailboat had fallen victim to his men's scoped and high-powered rifles over the years.

Gomez-Garcia knew he simply could not afford to let *anyone* return to civilization to talk about his escape route.

A few minutes later, the boat had slowly puttered out of the secluded inlet and was on its way down the river.

"Jaime," Gomez-Garcia said, turning to his lieutenant, "go below and bring a bottle of champagne and two glasses?"

Jaime glanced quickly from his boss to Michelle, then turned away.

Gomez-Garcia took Michelle's arm and led her to the rail as the yacht picked up speed on the water. A few minutes later, Jaime returned with an opened bottle of champagne and two stemmed glasses. He set the glasses on a deck table, poured them half full, then delivered them to the couple at the rail.

"Thank you, Jaime," the FARC leader said as he clinked his glass against Michelle's before taking a sip. "Now, if you would be so kind, would you bring me my machete?"

Jaime left on the new errand as Michelle said, "A machete? What on earth will you do with a machete on this boat?"

The men returned with the requested weapon, which he handed to his boss.

"I suppose I could tell you," the man said as he walked over to the table and set his champagne glass down before returning to the rail. "But it seems so cruel to do so. I think it is better that I just *show* you rather than tell you. You see, now that you are aware of my escape route, I can never allow you to live to tell about it."

Gomez-Garcia struck without warning and watched as Michelle's body slumped to the deck. He looked around for Jaime, intending to instruct the man to clean up the mess and dump the body he had enjoyed so much overboard. But his lieutenant was nowhere to be seen.

Antonio, however, had come up the ladder from the rooms below the deck, and he looked briefly at the dead woman next to the rail. "Ah," he said smiling. "So you are now Pepe 90, eh?"

"Of course not," Gomez-Garcia replied. "You know we never count the women."

Turning back to the rail as the boat continued through the water, Gomez-Garcia took a final look at Michelle.

It was a pity, he thought. She had been, as he had thought to many times before, a jaguar in bed. He turned toward the deck table to pour more champagne. It mattered little, he supposed, in the larger scope of things.

With his looks, money and power, there would always be other women to take her place.

16

"This curve up ahead," Wilson said as the van continued to speed across the gravel. "It's likely to be about
as good as it's gonna get."

"Then let's do it," Bolan said.

From the rear of the van, Cantu shouted, "Give me a
gun! Dammit, I can help you!"

"Yeah," Wilson said as he rounded the curve, then
stomped on the brake. "You'd help us all right. Then,
just as soon as the guys behind us were dead, you'd put
a bullet in both of our backs. No, thanks."

"Then what am I supposed to do?" the hit man yelled.

"If I were you," Bolan said, "I'd get down on the floor
and stay there."

The van skidded to halt just as the Plymouth
rounded the curve behind them. At the same time,
Bolan and Wilson grabbed an AK-47 and jumped out
of the van.

The bearded driver of the Plymouth was shocked to
see the van stop so suddenly. He stomped the brake
much as Wilson had done, doing his best to avoid a rear-
end collision. The car came sliding to a halt less than a
foot behind the van.

The Executioner and retired Texas Ranger opened up on the Plymouth at the same time, spraying full-auto streams of 7.62 mm rounds into the vehicle. The front tires blew and the front of the Plymouth dropped. The windshield shattered and behind the flying glass Bolan could see the driver and the other man in the front seat jerking violently as the high-powered rounds struck their chests.

Both men in the back seat of the Plymouth tried to get out. The one on Bolan's side of the vehicle had what looked like some kind of AR-15 clone gripped in both hands. He fell to another full-auto blast from the Executioner's AK-47.

But the AUC man on Wilson's side of the Plymouth made it out and behind the car while the retired Texas Ranger was still drilling rounds into the front seat. As the man darted for cover, he spread a wild shower of 7.62 mm NATO rounds from his H&K M-9l in the general direction of Bolan and Wilson. Crouching behind the car, he fell below the Executioner's field of vision as Bolan sent yet another burst of fire his way through the side of the Plymouth.

Wilson switched his point of aim a second later. But he was too late and the AUC man dropped down behind the rear bumper of the black Plymouth.

More rounds flying toward the van from behind the car told the Executioner that none of the bullets he had fired blindly through the side of the vehicle had found their mark.

"Rush him!" Bolan said quietly to Wilson. "It's the last thing he'll expect!"

Both men took off together, sprinting toward the Plymouth assault, rifles blasting away as they provided their own cover fire. The rounds coming toward them ceased as the AUC man was overwhelmed with sheer firepower. The Executioner and Wilson reached the rear of the Plymouth at the same time, catching the man crouched behind it in a cross fire that cast him first one way, then the other, and finally facedown on the ground.

Bolan's AK-47 locked open, empty, and he let the stock fall from his shoulder, still holding the fore end of the rifle in his left hand as he gripped Desert Eagle with his right. "Check the guys in the car," he told Wilson as he walked cautiously forward. Rolling the AUC man over, he knelt on one knee and looked at the glossy eyes as his index finger pressed against the man's carotid artery.

There was no pulse.

Bolan rose and joined Wilson, who was already back at the van. "You better take a look inside," the former blacksuit said, his face solemn.

The door on the passenger's side was still open and the Executioner stuck his head into the vehicle. There, in the back of the van, he saw Jose Cantu. The man lay on his side, his chest heaving up and down. Raising his eyes slightly, Bolan saw the round hole in the tinted glass of the rear window where one of the AUC man's wild rounds had drilled into the van.

"I told you to stay down," the Executioner said.

"I...wanted to...see," Cantu gasped.

Climbing inside the van, Bolan saw the entry wound in the hit man's chest. Cantu's eyes locked on the Executioner. "Am I...dying?" he asked, and a spray of pink came out of his mouth with the words.

"It looks like it," the Executioner said.

Cantu's eyes rolled upward. "*Madre de Dios*," he moaned. "Forgive my sins…." Then, looking back to Bolan, he said, "I have murdered many men and…I deserve this."

The Executioner nodded slowly.

"Perhaps…" the dying man breathed out. "I might…make…one last act of contrition?"

"What did you have in mind?" Bolan asked.

"My fingerprints," Cantu sputtered, spitting out more red froth as he did, "are on file with the CNP." Somehow, he found the strength to raise both hands. "And these will be…fresh. Take them." He closed his eyes for good and his chest rose and fell for the final time.

"Damn," Wilson said, shaking his head. "I'd never thought I'd feel sorry to see a scumbag like that go."

Bolan nodded. He understood. "There's a certain sadness to every wasted life," he said. "Worse when it's not only wasted but used for evil."

"Well," Wilson said, "at least he can do something good in death." Until then, both men had been watching Cantu's lifeless face. Now the Texan looked over to the Executioner. "Who's gonna do it?" he asked.

Bolan climbed back out of the van, preparing to circle the dead bodies and gather up the weapons. "You're the one with the big knife," he said.

"Thanks a lot."

"It's distasteful, but it's got to be done," Bolan said. "If you don't want to do it, give your bowie to me." He paused. "Like you said, it's one final act of good on the part of a man who lived for evil." The Executioner turned back to the open side door.

"Go on," Wilson said. "I'll do it. Maybe God'll take all this into consideration when He judges this heartless bastard."

"Maybe so," the Executioner said.

But he wouldn't have put any money on it.

17

"I'll be faxing Bear a set of Jose Cantu's fingerprints as soon as we get back to town, Barb," the Executioner said into the cell phone as Wilson guided the van back toward the highway leading into the city. "In the meantime, I need a team of blacksuits to fly down here in plain clothes. Make sure a couple of the guys have the same general descriptions as me and Wilson."

"How fast do you need them?" Price asked.

The Executioner looked at his watch. Even using the Learjet, the blacksuits were several hours away. He and Wilson would have to kill time after they'd completed the other things they had to do before they went back to Marquez's mansion. "As fast as possible," he said.

"Hang on a second," Price said. "I've got an idea."

Bolan heard a click as he was put on hold.

Bolan got a surprise a moment later when Price came back on the line. "I just talked to Phoenix Force," she said. "They've finished a job in southern Mexico and Jack's getting ready to pick them up to head back this way. Want them to handle it? They can get there a lot quicker."

"Affirmative," Bolan said. Phoenix Force was one of the other top counterterrorist teams that worked out of Stony Man. And their leader, David McCarter, and Canadian Gary Manning were big enough to pass for Bolan and Wilson during the few fast and furious seconds they might be visible to watchful eyes.

"I'll send them your way, then," Price said. "What else do they need to know?"

"Tell McCarter I need them to snatch up a Colombian National Police captain named Pedro Guttierez," the Executioner said. "Tell them to grab him in front of witnesses if they can. I need word of it to drift back to Marquez."

"This guy dirty?" Price asked.

"No, Barb," Bolan said. "Just the opposite. He's incorruptible according to Marquez, so the FARC man wants him dead." He paused a minute, knowing Price would already know what he was about to say next. He said it anyway. "Tell McCarter to sedate him and take him someplace out of the way until they hear from me. He's not to be hurt in any way."

"Affirmative, Striker. Anything else?"

"Yeah. Jack's not in the same plane he was in when he had to take off under gunfire when he dropped me off, is he?"

"No," she said. "He's in another Learjet with different markings. The one he flew you down in is getting a patch job for the bullet holes."

"Great," the Executioner said. "I want him to stand by at the airport. No one got a good look at his face— not even the customs man. As long as he uses another passport, he should be fine."

"Of course," Price said.

"Tell McCarter and his men to enter the country under the guise of oil speculators," Bolan said. "That's the most common reason Americans come down here."

"Will do."

"Tell Bear to stand by for the fax," Bolan repeated. "And I need to know just as soon as Phoenix Force takes Guttierez out of the picture."

"You got it," Price said. "Anything else?"

"Not at the moment." Bolan signed off and hung up.

The van reached the highway and turned south, toward Bogotá. Wilson kept the vehicle just below the speed limit and both men held their breath while they passed the same two CNP traffic control vehicles, still at the sides of the road. The van had so many bullet holes in it that it would stand out even in Colombia, and their first action when they got back to town would be to trade it for Wilson's Ford Explorer.

THE SHOPPING MALL parking lot was busy when Wilson pulled in an hour or so later. But even the more affluent patrons in the northern part of the city gave the bullet-riddled vehicle only casual second glances. He pulled up behind the Explorer and they transferred their equipment as quickly as possible before the blacksuit-trained man found an empty spot to dump the van for good.

Two minutes later, they were heading out toward the center of the city again.

"Where to first?" Wilson asked.

"We need to send the fax," the Executioner replied. "Find us an Internet café."

Wilson nodded and drove on. A few minutes later they saw what they needed and the retired Texas Ranger pulled into a small strip mall. Bolan and his partner got out of the van and started toward the door.

They had used a broken ballpoint pen to ink Cantu's fingers, then Bolan had rolled the impressions onto a clean white sheet of paper. Hand cleaner had then been used to wipe away the ink so Marquez would not see that prints had been taken.

The Executioner had the fingerprints hidden between other sheets of paper as they opened the door and entered the storefront.

The interior of the Internet café was alive with action, almost all of the computers lining the walls of the long narrow room occupied. Bolan spotted a modern fax machine in the far right-hand corner. Paying the attendant fifty pesos for its use, he kept the fingerprints covered until he reached the machine.

A minute later, the rolled impressions from the late Jose Cantu's fingers were on their way to Stony Man Farm. The Executioner had no way of controlling the records on his end of the fax. But the same sort of scrambler that was applied to all telephone calls into the Farm would insure that no one ever ran down the site to which the fax had been sent. And if anyone wanted to check on his end, it would be too late.

Bolan and Wilson would be long gone.

The Executioner led the way back to the Explorer, again taking the passenger's seat as Wilson dropped behind the wheel. Pulling out his cell phone, he tapped in the number to Stony Man Farm. A moment later Barbara Price answered. "Go, Striker," she said.

"We just sent the fax," he said. "Put me through to Bear, will you?"

Bolan heard a click and a moment later Kurtzman answered. "My fax machine is humming its tune right now," the computer whiz said.

"Good," Bolan said. "How fast can you get the prints switched?"

"I can classify Cantu's prints and switch the classifications in just a few minutes," Kurtzman said. "But as far as the actual fingerprint cards…well, I'm sure you see the problem there."

Bolan did, and he'd already thought of it. Switching the actual cards on which the impressions had been rolled would be a hands-on job. And he didn't have time to break into the CNP offices, find the files and get that done. But he doubted that Marquez's contact within the Colombian National Police would get out a magnifying glass and do a side-by-side comparison. It seemed far more likely that whoever it was would simply look to see that the classifications matched, and then tell the 14th Front leader that it was Pedro Guttierez's hands he had received from Bolan and Wilson.

"I know, Bear," Bolan said. "But we can only do what we can do."

"That's affirmative," the computer man said. "I've completed the job while we talked. Anybody who runs this fingerprint classification through the CNP computer files will come up with Pedro Guttierez's name."

"Thanks," Bolan said.

Barbara Price came back on the line. "Phoenix Force just touched down in Bogotá."

"Great," Bolan said. "Tell them to get on it, and get back with me as soon as Guttierez is out of the picture." He paused a second, then added, "Wilson and I will head toward Marquez's house. But we can't go in until we know that's happened."

"Okay," Price said. "I'll get things moving."

Bolan knew his plan to pass off Jose Cantu's fingerprints as those of Captain Guttierez had holes in it— big holes. But he had been unable to come up with anything better, and that was just the way things went sometimes. You weighed the situation, considered all of the facts, then took calculated risks.

"Let's go see our friend Marquez," he said to Wilson.

THEY HAD REACHED the affluent neighborhood where Marquez lived, and been waiting in the parking lot of another shopping mall for thirty minutes, when Bolan's cell phone began to vibrate in his pocket. "Hello, Barb," he said.

"Not unless I've had a sex change operation, mate," David McCarter said by way of greeting.

"I wouldn't advise it, David," Bolan said. "You still wouldn't look as good as Barbara."

"Not quite," McCarter quipped back. "But this call is not to discuss my anatomy. It's to tell you that we nabbed your boy."

"Great," the Executioner said. "Give me the details in case I need them."

"Went right to the source," McCarter said. "Got him walking down the steps of CNP headquarters with quite a bit of fanfare, as a matter of fact."

"Anybody hurt?" Bolan asked.

"No," McCarter said. "Not a shot fired."

"So who actually might have been seen?" Bolan asked.

"Yours truly and Gary," McCarter came back. "We were only in sight for a second or two. Manning laid the man out with one of those Canadian pile-driving lumberjack punches of his, then we carried him to the van. There was a good deal of screaming, but it appeared to be nothing but citizens out front at the time. Like I said, not a soul shot at us."

Bolan nodded. The men of Phoenix Force were not only professional warriors, they were true friends. As they had done so many times in the past, they had risked their lives to help him without even so much as knowing why. "Okay," the Executioner said. "Is he awake yet?"

"Oh no," the Phoenix Force leader advised. "Calvin fired him up with a dose of Demerol as soon as we pulled away. He'll be dreaming peacefully for some time."

Bolan's thoughts drifted to Calvin James, another member in good standing of the Phoenix Force team. The former U.S. Navy SEAL was a highly trained medic as well as a top-notch fighting man. "Sounds like you did a good job," he said. "Exactly when did all this go down?"

"About a half hour ago," McCarter said.

The Executioner looked at his watch. The CNP headquarters were a forty-five minute drive from Marquez's mansion. If he allowed time to cover finding a place to kill Guttierez—and collect the nauseating evidence the 14th Front FARC man had insisted on—they should be able to show up at the gate in another half hour or so.

"Thanks," Bolan said. "Just find a place to keep him out of sight for a while. When this is all over, you can drop him off someplace and he'll be no worse for wear."

"Right," McCarter said. "Let us know if we can do anything else."

"Will do." Bolan hung up.

Wilson had heard enough of the one-sided conversation to know Guttierez was safely out of the way. "We're running a little low on gas," he said. "I better find a filling station."

Bolan nodded as they pulled out of the parking lot. The retired Texas Ranger drove them to a store with gas pumps in the front. The men filled up and took the opportunity to eat the first meal they'd had in more than a day. As he was swallowing the last mouthful of his sandwich, the Executioner glanced at his wristwatch.

"Let's go," he told Wilson. "By the time we get there, it'll be about right."

The blacksuit-trained man nodded. Twisting the key, he fired the Explorer back to life and pulled out onto the street again.

18

The uniformed man at the guard shack outside Marquez's mansion was the same sentry who had been on duty, when Bolan and Wilson had gone to the house with Cantu. He recognized them, and took the Desert Eagle, Beretta, and "Becky" and "Betty" through the window without making the men get out of the Explorer. But when the guns were safely in the guard shack, he said, "Where is the big knife?"

"Ah, sorry," Wilson said. "Forgot all about old Bonnie." He leaned forward in the driver's seat and pulled the bowie—still in its sheath—from behind his back and handed it to the guard. "Take good care of her, *amigo*," he told the man. "She's been a member of the family for a long time."

"*Sí,* I understand," the guard said. He looked down at the big blade, obviously fascinated by it, as he manipulated the control in the guard shack and the iron gates in front of the van began to swing inward.

The retired Texas Ranger parked in front of the main door in the circular drive. Bolan got out, opened the rear door and lifted the ice chest off of the back seat.

Bolan and Wilson were met at the door by the same deaf and bald giant they had seen the day before. He stepped back and ushered them into the foyer before leading them back to the metal detector. Still carrying the North American Arms .380 and the Black Widow .22 Magnum guns, both Bolan and Wilson triggered the buzzer as they passed through. But this time, remembering Cantu's rant about them both carrying shrapnel, the armed men just waved them on. Once again, Bolan was reminded of how well Jose Cantu had been able to think on his feet. He wished that such a mind had been put into service to help others instead of to murder them.

They were escorted to where Marquez stood behind his desk. The FARC man's smile reached from one ear to the other. "You work fast, it seems," he told them. "Only a few minutes ago I received word that Guttierez had been abducted." He laughed and shook his head. "You have *cojones*, my friends. Right in front of CNP headquarters? I am amazed. Truly amazed." He laughed again.

Bolan set the cooler on the desk and looked at his watch. "Grabbed him about an hour ago," he said. "Little more, maybe." He looked up at the FARC man who was now extending his hand in congratulations. Gripping it, the Executioner said, "I saw no reason to waste time."

"*Muy bien, muy bien,*" Marquez said gleefully. "May I assume you have brought me the head?"

Wilson stepped in with his Texas drawl. "Pretty sure you wouldn't of wanted it," he said. "Very, very, messy. In fact, we had to ditch the van we used for the grab." He paused, chuckled, then said, "Good thing we stole it, huh?"

Marquez nodded, then lifted the lid off the ice chest. He looked at the contents for a moment, then pressed a button on the phone on his desk and lifted the receiver. "Manuel," he said. "please come to my office immediately."

Hanging up, he said, "As you know, I would have preferred the head."

"I tried," the Executioner said. "But like I told you, sometimes things like this just take their own course."

Marquez nodded. "At least you are honest," he said. Suddenly, he frowned, as if something he should have noticed earlier had just hit him. "Where is Jose?" he asked.

Bolan cleared his throat. "He's already taken off for parts unknown," he said. "I don't know exactly what's got him so spooked but, like he told you yesterday, he's convinced that either the law, or somebody else, is going to get him." Clearing his throat again, he added, "To tell you the truth, Señor Marquez, while he didn't actually come right out and say it, I think he's a little afraid of you, too. He didn't even stick around to get his part of the money, and wouldn't give us an address to send it to, either."

Marquez shrugged. "He had no reason to worry about me," the FARC man said. "I have always been pleased with his work." He opened the humidor and took out three Churchills cigars, handing one each to Bolan and Wilson. "Did he even help you with Guttierez?"

"He gave us a hand," the retired Texas Ranger said with a straight face. "But then he took off. Now, about the money...." Wilson let his voice trail off.

"*Sí, sí,*" Marquez said. "Just as soon as I am able to prove that the hands I just saw belonged to the captain, you will be paid. And then I will have another job for you if you're interested."

"We're always interested," Bolan said as the office door opened behind him. He looked over his shoulder to see one of Marquez's men enter.

Marquez pointed to the ice chest. "You know what to do," he said.

The underling nodded, slung the sling attached to his machine pistol over his neck, and lifted the ice chest. A moment later he was gone again.

"Please," Marquez said. "Gentlemen, sit down. Enjoy your cigars. This will not take more than a half hour, I am sure, and then you will receive your money." He lifted the same gold lighter Bolan remembered from the last time they'd been in the office and handed it to Wilson.

The retired Ranger lit his cigar, then Bolan lit his and handed the lighter back to their host.

The Executioner sat silently, pleased that Marquez had assured them it would take no longer than thirty minutes. That had to mean that Marquez would be satisfied with a quick comparison of the fingerprints on file.

After only twenty minutes had passed Marquez's man stuck his head in the door and nodded.

"Ah," Marquez said, rising to shake both men's hands. "It appears you have passed the test. The fingerprints do indeed belong to *el capitano,* and he will no longer be a thorn in my side." Turning around, he lifted a painting of a mountain landscape off the wall to reveal a large safe. Covering the dial with his body, he twisted the combination into the device and a moment later the door popped open.

Bolan and Wilson watched him reach inside and pull out several stacks of U.S. currency, wrapped in paper bands. He set them on desk, counted out twenty-five thousand dollars for each man, then another twenty-five. Replacing the rest of the money in the safe, he closed the door and re-hung the landscape. "Jose's share," he said. "It can be divided between you, or given to him if you ever see him again." He sat back in his chair behind the desk.

Bolan and Wilson stuffed the money in various pockets and prepared to leave. Marquez motioned for them to sit back down. *"Por favor,"* the 14th Front man said. "As you will remember, I told you I had another job for you."

Bolan and Wilson sat.

"As you know, Jose carried out assassinations for me to which I did not want to be connected," Marquez said. "And the one I have in mind next is not only one to which I do not want to be connected, it is one to which I cannot afford to ever be suspected of taking part in."

The Executioner and retired Texas Ranger listened as the FARC man told them who he wanted killed next.

Bolan kept the poker face he had been wearing. "This one is going to be even harder than Captain Guttierez," he told Marquez.

"That is why I am prepared to pay you each one million U.S. dollars to carry it out," the 14th Front leader replied.

Bolan knew when to bluff. "What do you say we make it two million each," he said politely. "Once this job is over, you're going to be the most powerful man in your whole organization. Four million bucks will seem like pocket change to you."

Marquez threw back his head and laughed. "You remind me of Jose," he said. "Always trying to squeeze me for a little more, no matter how much I offer."

Bolan let a thin smile creep over his face. "That's the name of the game in our business, Señor Marquez," he said. "Get all you can while you can. Because the time comes—just like it now has for our friend Jose—when it's time to call it quits and disappear from the playing field all together."

Marquez stopped laughing but still grinned. "You

are correct, of course," he said. "Both in stating that people in your line of work have a limited career span, and the fact that I can afford to pay you two million each. Consider it done." He stood up once more and extended his hand to confirm the verbal contract.

The Executioner and Wilson rose as well, taking turns shaking the FARC man's hand. "I have just one more question," Bolan said.

Marquez answered by tilting his head slightly to the side and waiting.

"Do you have a man—someone you can trust—who can introduce us to the mark?" A connection had begun gnawing in the back of the Executioner's brain. But all he knew at the moment was that it had something to do with the inside man Marquez had used to run the fingerprint comparison.

Marquez frowned and shook his head. "Yes and no," he said. "Yes, in that I know a man who could easily pave the way for you. No, however, in the fact that I will not use him for that purpose." He paused to lean down and roll the ash off the end of his cigar into the ashtray. "This man has, shall we say, questionable loyalties. He has worked for me and the man you are about to kill. And, as I have said, I cannot afford to have any trail whatsoever that leads back to me on all of this. Not even within—no, let me change that, *particularly* within— our organization. Besides, for two million dollars each, you can afford to find, and pay, your own informants."

The Executioner understood and nodded in agreement. "It was worth asking," he said. He and Wilson turned and walked toward the door. As he grasped the knob, Marquez called them back.

Bolan and Wilson turned to face him.

Marquez had a wide smile on his face. "Perhaps I should not tell you," he said. "But I was ready to go to five million each for this job."

Bolan chuckled. "Guess I'd better sharpen up on my bargaining skills," he said, then opened the door and led Wilson out into the hall. The men exchanged quick glances before the bald giant reappeared to escort them out of the mansion. Neither man spoke as they walked back to the car. But Bolan was reminded that while a warrior such as he had to make his own luck, once in a while a break came along.

The man Marquez wanted killed was Carlos Gomez-Garcia.

Pepe 89.

19

Like all of the Executioner's missions, this one had been fast and furious. But it was about to speed up to a whole new level of intensity.

Bolan was back on the line to Barbara Price at Stony Man Farm as soon as Marquez's mansion was out of sight. "First," he told the mission controller, "our friend Jose Cantu won't be needing the ten grand you wired down to him after all. But I will. Can you change the name on the transfer?"

Price was silent for a moment, then said, "It might raise some curious eyebrows on your end, Striker. The best thing is to just let it revert after three days like we agreed earlier. I can do another, separate, wire a lot easier, and less suspiciously. How much do you want, and what name do you want it in this time?"

Bolan thought for a moment, then said, "Send fifty-thousand dollars this time in Paul Wilson's name. Since neither of us have accounts there, they're going to ask for eighteen different kinds of identification. He'll have it."

"Consider it done," Price said. "I'm typing it in as we speak.

"Next," Bolan said. "When was the last time the CNP or Colombian military tried to hit Pepe 89's ranch?"

"Funny you should ask," Price said. "The Junglas have another search going on there right now. As usual, Pepe and all of the men who have outstanding warrants have disappeared into thin air. Just the house staff and a few cattle and sheep herders still around."

Bolan looked at his watch. "Then contact Jack and tell him we're headed for the airport as soon as we leave the bank. And get hold of Hal. See if he can't put a little pressure on the DEA agent-advisers who'll have gone in with the military. I need them to stall that search long enough for Wilson and I to get into the air over the ranch."

"Hal will be the first call I make when we hang up."

"Okay," Bolan went on as Wilson pulled up in front of the bank. Patting a back pocket of his blue jeans to make sure his passport and billfold were in place, he jumped out of the Explorer and hurried inside. "As soon as we're over the ranch," Bolan said. "I'll let you know. But we'll be flying high—too high to be seen on the ground, which also means too high for us to see when the Black Hawks leave again. So I'll need immediate communication from you when the choppers are gone." He paused, a thousand thoughts racing through his mind at the same time. "Wilson and I are going to jump in, and we've got to do it *after* the military is gone but *before* Pepe and his 'band of forty thieves' come home."

"Okay," Price said. "What else?"

"Give me Bear," he said.

As he waited, Wilson came out of the bank carrying a large zippered canvas bag. He got back behind the wheel, then backed out of the parking lot onto the street again.

A moment later, Kurtzman said. "What's up, Striker?"

"I've got a hunch I'd like you to follow up on," Bolan

said. "Can you get the phone records of both Gomez-Garcia and Ramon Marquez?"

"Like taking candy from a baby," the computer wizard told him.

"Then get them, will you, Bear?" Bolan said as Wilson drove toward the airport. "Cross-reference them and see if there are any of the same incoming and outgoing calls to the same numbers. Particularly if those numbers lead back to any Colombian government buildings."

There was a pause on Kurtzman's end. "You think Marquez and Pepe 89 have the same inside man?"

"I don't know," Bolan said. He remembered what Marquez had said about having a man who could get them to Pepe 89 but being afraid of that man's true loyalties. "Like I said, it's a hunch. But it's worth checking out."

"I'll get right on it," Kurtzman said. "I'll call you when I find anything."

"Thanks, Bear. Now, let me talk to Barbara one more time."

A click later, Price said, "More, Striker?"

"No," Bolan said. "Just stand by. I'll call you again when we get close to the ranch." He was about to hang up when Kurtzman broke into the line.

"Striker," the computer man said. "You still there?"

"Affirmative."

"Okay, here's something very interesting. There are multiple calls, both to and from, a line that traces back to the office of the president of Colombia."

For a moment, the line went silent as the Executioner's mind went to work on this unexpected development. Could the Colombian president himself be the leak? The drug runners of the nation certainly made far more money than he did, and most men had their price. Besides, Colombian politicians were even more notorious for dishonesty than their counterparts around the world.

No, Bolan realized as the airport's high, concertina-wire-topped chain link perimeter fence appeared in the distance. That still didn't make sense. If the Colombian president was on the take, why would he call the U.S. and ask for help? It would only draw more attention to the drug smuggling and other atrocities of the FARCs than they already had. "You find anything else?" Bolan finally asked.

"Just that most, but not all, of the calls are at night. After normal business hours." Again, there was a pause, then Kurtzman added, "But like I said, there are exceptions."

"And my guess is that those exceptions will match up to the dates when the cops or army raided the ranch," the Executioner said. "Try matching them up. Obviously, the inside man feels more comfortable talking at night. But when Pepe's about to be raided, he has to take the risk of being caught."

"Hang on." The line went silent except for the tap of keyboard keys on Kurtzman's end. Then Kurtzman said, "Bingo. The day calls are early morning. On the same dates as past raids by the military or police."

"Thanks," Bolan said as Wilson pulled the Explorer into the airport and began taking the narrow drive that led to the private plane landing strips. "We'll talk again soon."

"I won't be going anywhere," Kurtzman said and hung up

Wilson found a parking place near the landing strips and killed the Explorer's engine. Quickly, they disassembled the AK-47s enough to hide in the retired Texas Ranger's equipment bags, then carried them toward the Learjet waiting to taxi onto the runway.

The same customs man who had greeted them upon their entry to the country was talking to Grimaldi through the pilot's open door as they approached. The conversation looked friendly if the expression on Grimaldi's face was any indication. But if there was going to be a problem, this is when it would come, the Executioner realized as they drew nearer to the plane.

The customs official was the only man who had actually seen Grimaldi's face. And while Bolan might be clean shaved and dark-haired rather than blond and bearded, with both he and Wilson dressed considerably differently than they had been during the initial gunfight, there was little doubt that this man would know who he was dealing with again.

But the customs man only smiled as they stepped up to the plane and began stowing their equipment bags in the luggage compartment. Bolan could see whatever bills Grimaldi had already given the man sticking out of the corner of one of his uniform pockets. The Executioner and Wilson climbed aboard the Learjet, and a moment later the plane was in the air.

Bolan had barely strapped himself in when the cell phone in his pocket vibrated.

"Well, Striker, I suggest you strike fast," Price said as the plane began to gain altitude. "The Colombian Junglas have been stalled as long as they can be." The mission controller paused for a breath, then finished with, "The Black Hawks are warming up right now and their estimated time of departure is twenty minutes."

"Thanks," Bolan said and hung up again.

Turning to Grimaldi, he said, "They're leaving the ranch in twenty, Jack. Better kick it into high gear."

Stony Man Farm's top pilot nodded as they continued to rise. "And *you*, my friends," he said, "had better get your jumpin' jackets on."

Bolan nodded, stood and cut between the seats to the rear of the plane.

Wilson was already at the lockers, pulling out a pair of parachutes.

20

The Learjet could risk only one low pass over the ranch. Bolan made the most of it, eyeing the property through binoculars as Grimaldi cut the engine to the slowest speed the craft could tolerate and still stay in the air. Below, the Executioner could see the house, swimming pool, lawn, and the herds of cattle and sheep grazing on the plateaus and in the valleys behind the cliffside mansion. Below the steep cliff on the other side of the house stood the jungle.

The Black Hawk helicopters were still where they had landed, on the lawn adjacent to the patio surrounding the pool area.

The jet flew north, as if passing the ranch had simply been part of a flight pattern to Sogomoso, a small city several miles farther in the distance. Then Grimaldi took them high into the clouds before turning the Learjet around.

The plane stayed hidden in the billowy whiteness over the northern Cordillera Oriental mountains as it made its way south again. But the ranch, and the Black Hawks, were hidden from view. The Executioner would have to rely on the readings of Grimaldi's Global Positioning System and the voice-intel of Barbara Price and Aaron Kurtzman who were watching the ranch via satellite.

Finally, the cell phone vibrated again and Bolan, already wearing his parachute with a small backpack and another, larger bag strapped to his body, held the instrument to his ear. "Go, Barb," the Executioner said.

"The first of the choppers just took off," the mission controller told him.

"Okay," Bolan replied. "Stay on the line. Let me know when they're all gone."

Several minutes ticked by as Grimaldi continued to keep to the tightest flight pattern the Learjet would allow, directly overhead. Finally, after what seemed like hours, Price said, "Bear's waving at me through the glass, Striker. Now he's giving me the thumbs-up. The Black Hawks are all gone and you're good to go."

"Affirmative," the Executioner said. "Thanks. See you when I get back."

Bolan hung up and dropped the phone back into his pocket. In addition to donning their parachutes and other gear, he and Wilson had changed into blacksuits from the Learjet's lockers. The two warriors had also traded their AK-47s for M-16 assault rifles, and both still toted their handguns of choice. Wilson also had his sawed-off 12-gauge, and he wasn't going anywhere without Bonnie.

The larger bag Bolan had strapped to his body contained another weapon he'd found in one of the lockers on board the Learjet. He had no idea whether or not it would be needed but, his instincts told him it was worth bringing along. And he knew it would be better to have it and not use it than to need it and not have it.

Raising his voice slightly so Grimaldi could hear him in the front of the plane, Bolan said, "Anytime now, Jack. We want our feet to touch down as close to the house as possible."

Grimaldi turned halfway in his seat. "I'll do what I can," he said. "But keep in mind, the place is on the side of a cliff. The wind catches you, and you overshoot, you'll be a day and a half climbing back up out of the jungle on the other side."

Bolan had seen the jungle below the cliff as they flew over. Grimaldi was right. They couldn't afford to drift past the cliff. "Then if we have to err, Jack, let's err on the front side of the house. I'd rather land in a herd of those cattle or sheep than end up down below."

"Damn," Wilson said. "Cattle and sheep? I left Texas to get away from all that."

Bolan shook his head. Before he could reply, Grimaldi had shouted, "Ten seconds, gentlemen."

A few moments later Bolan and the retired Texas Ranger were plummeting toward the earth.

They had planned a HALO—High Altitude Low Opening—jump to keep from drawing more attention than was necessary, and both chutes opened flawlessly. As they floated through the air, Bolan eyed the grounds below. At least ten thousand cattle grazed on the grassy plateaus and in the several valleys behind the hillside mansion, with herds of sheep in others. Closer to the house was a small pen packed with swine. To the casual observer, the ranch appeared to be nothing more than the operation of a wealthy Colombian man of the land. Even the landing strip on one of the plateaus could be attributed to the take-offs and landings of an agro-businessman's private plane.

There was no indication that the site's true purpose was to house the mastermind of one of the most ruthless terrorist organizations in the world.

People began to appear like ants below, and as they

fell closer Bolan could see that a few of the men were walking away from the house toward pickups and ancient flatbed trucks. Those would be the employees tending the livestock, who would have been rounded up by the invading Junglas on the off chance that one or more of the wanted FARC men had been caught at the site and was trying to conceal himself among the lawful workers. But as the Executioner and Wilson fell even closer, the men stopped next to their vehicles and looked up, watching their descent, and more than likely assuming there was a second wave of attack to catch Pepe 89 and his FARC men coming back to the house.

So unconcerned were the ranch workers that they began to move toward the spot where it appeared Bolan and Wilson would finally land, and when the Executioner's black nylon combat boots finally came down on the lawn several yards from the swimming pool, at least a dozen men in torn shirts, overalls and ragged straw hats were waiting. Wilson hit twenty yards behind him a few seconds later, and both men began rolling up their chutes.

The employees waited, certain that the two men were with either the Colombian military or police. They were probably happy to have their backbreaking work interrupted a little longer, and Bolan saw no reason to tell them any differently—at least not until he had them all assembled at the house again. Knowing that while his Spanish was nearly flawless, his accent would give him away, he kept his words to the bare minimum. Pointing toward the house, he simply said, "*Vamanos!*"

The workers began trudging toward the house. Now and then, one or two of them would look up at the sky, probably wondering when the other parachuting troops would come.

By the time they had reached the pool, a man wearing a servant's uniform and a crisp white apron had come out of the house. He was followed by a half-dozen other house employees, the men dressed similarly and the women wearing the black-and-white uniforms of maids.

"That is Juan," the old man said, pointing a crooked index finger at the man in the apron.

Juan walked forward, his shoulders back, his head upright. "I was given to believe we were finished," he said, stopping a foot in front of Bolan and Wilson. "At least for today."

"Not yet," Bolan said. He pulled his arms out of the small backpack he had worn under his chute and opened the top, producing the zippered money bag Wilson had gotten at the bank. "How many of you are there here, Juan?" the Executioner asked.

"Employees, you mean?" Juan asked.

"Yes. I'm not interested in Pepe, or the men who fled with him. At least not right now. How many *innocent* people work here. Like you."

"Twenty-seven," Juan said, the quickness of his reply telling the Executioner he had probably just answered the same question for the military men a few minutes earlier.

Bolan unzipped the bag and pulled out a fistful of notes. There were gasps among the waiting workers, and even Juan raised his eyebrows. Handing one of the bills to the man in the apron, the Executioner said, "Tell everyone to line up. I've got some for each of them."

Juan cleared his throat, then said, "Please, do not toy with these people. They have worked like beasts of burden all of their lives, and are deeper in debt now than the day they were born."

"I'm not toying with them," the Executioner said. "I

really am going to hand these out, and even more later. Have them line up."

Juan shrugged and called out to the men and women who were still chattering about what they had just seen. He told them to form a single line. There were more gasps when he advised them that they would all receive money as he just had.

One man, wearing a torn and patched khaki shirt, with a hand-rolled cigarette hanging out of his mouth, shouted, "Wait, my friends! Nothing is ever free!"

Then, turning to Bolan, he said, "What is it we must do for this money?"

Bolan turned to him. "Nothing. It's yours to keep no matter what you do." He paused. "But there is more for everyone, too. And if you do what I ask, you'll each receive almost two thousand dollars in U.S. currency."

Silence fell over the assembled workers. Some, Bolan could see, were simply stunned by the amount which was far more than any of them would earn in a year. But on the faces of others, he saw that they had no more idea how much money it was. "Translate that into pesos for them, Juan," the Executioner said.

Juan did. And the gasps became oaths of astonishment. But the same doubter with the patched shirt and cigarette asked again, "Yes, but what is it we must do for you to get this money?"

"It's more about what I want you *not* to do," Bolan said. "I want you to keep quiet about us being here when Pepe and his men get back. Just go about your normal chores like you always would. We'll take care of the rest."

"And if we don't?" the man with the hand-rolled cigarette asked skeptically.

The Executioner shrugged. "You won't get any more

money. But I should warn you, one way or another, there won't be any jobs here tomorrow. Pepe 89 and all of his men are going to be dead."

More chattering began among the servants and field employees. Then one of the women dressed as a maid stepped forward. "Señor," she said, "you do not understand. Pepe will kill us if we cooperate with you."

"We live each day in fear for our lives," a sun-beaten man in a crumbling straw hat said. "The slightest infraction can bring on death from our employer. His machetes are a constant threat. Each day we wonder which of us will be responsible for a new number after his name."

"Only yesterday," another said, "he beheaded one of his own top men—a man who had been his friend since childhood."

Bolan looked out over the frightened, downtrodden people. "This is your chance to change all that," he said. "I'm giving you the chance to get out of here and create new lives for yourselves. But I can't supply you with the courage it'll take for you to trust me. That's up to you." He looked to Wilson. "My friend and I are going to go over here by the swimming pool for a few minutes to let you talk it over. But we don't have long to wait. Make no mistake—we're going to kill Pepe 89 and his men before we leave here today. But we've got to be in position before they get back. Make your decision quickly." Without another word, the Executioner and retired Texas Ranger walked out of earshot.

Less than a minute later Juan shouted, "Señors!"

Bolan and Wilson returned to the group.

"We have voted," Juan said. "And all of us except Santiago here, came quickly to the agreement that we should do as you suggest. And now, even Santiago votes

our way." Both times he said "Santiago" he had indi-
cated the man with the hand-rolled cigarette and patched
shirt. Santiago stared at the ground.

"What changed his mind?" Bolan asked.

Juan smiled. "We told him that if he ruined this opportunity for the rest of us we would cut his heart out
and feed it to the pigs," he said, pointing toward the pig-
pen in the distance.

"Ain't democracy great?" Wilson said with a
straight face.

Bolan took the zippered bank bag out of his pack.
"Do you all trust Juan?" he asked the crowd.

All of the heads nodded.

"Then I'll give him the rest of the money to divide
up among you," Bolan said. "My friend and I are going
to find a place to hide."

"If you please," Juan said, holding up a hand. "I think
I have a better idea."

Bolan looked at him quizzically.

"If you wait for Pepe to return to this house, many
of his men will have dispersed in other directions. You
will get Pepe and probably Jaime and Antonio, his two
top men. But most of the others will escape you."

"So what's your idea?" the Executioner asked.

"Hold on to your money for a few more minutes,"
Juan said, the smile still strong on his face. "And I will
show you a secret. It is a secret of which Pepe does not
know I am aware." Turning on his heels, he said, "Follow me, *por favor*."

Bolan stuffed the money bag back in his pack and he
and Wilson followed the man into the house, to the pantry
just off the kitchen. Juan lifted a huge can of pinto beans
and the hidden panel swung open to reveal a passageway.

"It leads to a walled-off portion of the basement," Juan said. "There, you must remove a stone from the wall to gain access to another tunnel. The stone is about this high." He raised a hand to eye level, then went on. "And about the size of a baseball. If you know what to look for, you will see it."

"Where does the other tunnel go?" Bolan asked the man.

Juan shrugged and blushed slightly. "I do not know," he said. "I have never worked up the courage to go beyond that point."

Bolan nodded his understanding and handed over the money bag. He had to agree—Juan's plan was, indeed, better than his own of just hiding in the house and waiting.

"Is there anything else you need, Juan?" Wilson asked just before he and the Executioner started into the tunnel.

"I ask only one more thing," Juan said. Now, the smile was gone, and his face was stern and hard. "Make sure the *bustard's* name never becomes Pepe 90."

21

The Executioner tapped the Stony Man Farm number into the cell phone as he left the tunnel. "We're in position, Barb," he whispered, as he hurriedly took up hiding behind a large boulder just outside the exit. He watched Wilson secrete himself just as quickly within the thick leaves and vines of the foliage that began only a few feet beyond the mountain.

Both men had a clear view of the dock within the secluded inlet just off the Cusiana River. Bolan was tempted to walk down and check it out further. But he had no idea when Gomez-Garcia and his men might return. And he didn't want to take the chance of giving them advance warning should they appear suddenly.

"Affirmative, Striker, " Price said on the other end of the line. "Hal got hold of the Man, who called the Colombian president. The phone line into his office—the one both Marquez and Pepe 89 have been getting calls from—turns out to be one Colombia's top man didn't even know existed. It actually runs into a janitor's closet."

"If I was the president of Colombia," Bolan whispered into the instrument, "I'd be checking into any FARC connections my custodians might have." The answer to the leak, it appeared, had been so simple that the

Colombian president had overlooked it. A janitor undoubtedly cleaned the presidential offices every night, which was when the majority of calls were made. All it would take for the FARC janitor to learn about both military or police attacks on Pepe 89's ranch would be a few notes or papers carelessly left on el president's desk.

"Unless the Colombian president is really careless," he told Price, "he's bound to have at least one of his security men in his office when the janitor goes in, doesn't he?"

"He does," Price said. "Which makes it look like his security team is getting paid off, too. It should be fairly easy to figure out when this is over and they start cracking down."

"I'd find out who pays the phone bill, too," the Executioner said. "That person's bound to have known about the hidden line in the closet, too."

"That's exactly what's going to happen eventually," Price said. "But right now, the Man has convinced his Colombian counterpart not to spook Pepe and his men before you get a chance to take them out. Bear has been monitoring that phone line and—" Her voice suddenly halted. "Stand by, Striker. Bear's waving at me through the glass again."

Bolan heard a click as he was put on hold.

A second later, Price was back. "They finally picked up traffic on the line," she said. "It was the janitor making a call. He's given the all clear to Pepe to return to the house."

"Well," the Executioner said, "we'll make sure he gets a good reception. Did the Bear get a location on them? Any idea how long we've got before they show up?"

"Negative, Striker," Price said. "But he said there was background noise during the call—sounds he doubted came from any janitor's closet. Wait a minute—he's got more."

Price was back on in another few seconds. "He just ran the recording of the call through a computer sound-ID program. The background noise was the sound of a marine engine for a medium-sized motor yacht passing through water at high speed. So they're on their way."

Bolan nodded. Juan had never had the courage to explore the hidden passageway he'd found, but it only made sense that after they came out of the tunnel the men of the 28th Front would escape, then return, by boat. And the dock connecting the land to the water confirmed that theory.

A moment later the Executioner heard the sound of a marine engine in the distance. "That's it, Barb," he said into the phone. "I can hear them coming now."

"Be careful, Striker," Price said.

"Aren't I always?" Bolan said and hung up. Quickly, he double-checked his M-16, the Beretta and Desert Eagle, and the TOPS SAW knife he had transferred to the nylon web belt around the waist of his blacksuit. He had opened the large canvas bag and had been assembling the other weapon he'd brought from the Learjet while he talked to Price, and now he primed it and set it down next to him behind the boulder. "You hear them?" he whispered to Wilson.

"I hear them," the retired Texas Ranger said softly from inside the leaves and vines. "Only problem I've got is which gun to shoot first."

Bolan waited as the roar of the engine grew louder. "From what Juan told us," he said, "it sounds like not all of them will be getting off here. We'll have to wait and see before we know our exact battle plan."

Through the greenery, he heard Wilson laugh softly. "This reminds me of a lot of nights hiding along the Rio Grande," he said. "Waiting on drug smugglers and sundry other miscreants to cross into the U.S. Our battle plan was always pretty much the same."

"What was that?" Bolan asked.

"Stand up and shoot 'em," the retired Texas Ranger said.

"Just don't stand up too tall," Bolan said.

"Don't worry," Wilson replied. "I'm not *that much* Texan."

"Okay, quiet now," Bolan warned as the boat suddenly appeared on the water beyond the dock. He heard the engine die down to a soft purr as the hull came into view. There were at least twenty men on board the yacht, and the barrels of the rifles pointed up at the sky.

Bolan waited. He figured if he had any brains at all, Gomez-Garcia would know that if anyone was onto his escape route, Bolan's location was where they would lie in wait. That meant he'd have his men on high alert until they knew the coast was clear. But there was nothing the Executioner could do about that. The best strategy was still to wait until Pepe, and whoever was getting off at this stop with him, disembarked, then open fire. He looked down at the weapon on the canvas bag at his side.

He was glad his gut had told him to bring it. There was every chance in the world it would be needed.

The boat pulled up to the dock and a man wearing an anchor-crested captain's hat hopped off the deck, onto the wood, and began wrapping a line around one of the metal cleats at his feet. A moment later, four men with 9 mm Uzi submachine guns followed him onto the dock. From hiding, Bolan watched their eyes scan back

and forth through the mountains, looking for any sign
of a trap. A few yards away, the Executioner knew Wilson had seen the same thing.

Then, a sudden upward glance by one of the men put
Bolan's senses on high alert. He watched as a flash of
reflected sunlight came down from two sites in the high
rocks on the other side of the inlet. Then the man turned
to look almost directly above the Executioner's head,
waited, then nodded.

Though he couldn't see it, Bolan knew that another
mirror signal had just come down from above him.

Snipers. Gomez-Garcia had snipers stationed at three
sites in the rocks above them. The only reason the men
hadn't seen Bolan and Wilson was because the two warriors had gone into hiding immediately upon leaving the
tunnel. Had he gone down to check out the dock as he'd
been tempted to do, Bolan knew that he'd have been
dead before he even knew the men were there.

"You see that?" Wilson whispered softly through
the leaves.

"Yes. Quiet," Bolan whispered back. Rising just over
the boulder, the Executioner continued to watch the
men with the Uzis. Two more men, packing only side
arms on their belts, dropped down off the deck next.
They turned back and helped a man wearing a white
shirt, dark slacks and black wraparound sunglasses onto
land. This man wore no weapon except a machete with
a wooden handle wrapped in copper wire.

It was the Executioner's first sight of Carlos Gomez-Garcia. His jaw tightened as he determined it would also
be his last.

As soon as Pepe 89 was safely on the dock, the man
in the captain's cap unwrapped the line, then hopped

back up on deck. The rifle barrels on board still pointed at the air. But it was obvious that the men holding the weapons were still on alert as the yacht began backing away from the dock.

The Executioner felt his jaw tighten further. The snipers had thrown a crimp into his plan, but he knew he could not afford to let that stop him. He'd never get a better chance to wipe out Pepe and the entire 28th Front, and he might never get another chance at all. He and Wilson would have to risk the sniper fire, relying on movement and concealment to keep from getting shot.

"You ready?" the Executioner whispered to the hidden man.

"As ready as I'm gonna get," Wilson said. "This new sniper crap really sucks, you know?"

"I know," Bolan said softly. "It means that one of us has got to concentrate on them while the other fires at the men on the dock and the boat."

"I've got a clear shot at one of the snipers on the other side of the water," Wilson said. "I can even see him."

Bolan could not see either of the men across the water from behind the boulder, and neither of them knew exactly where the one above their heads had set up his "hide."

"How about the other one over there?" he asked.

"Haven't a clue," Wilson said.

"At least you've got a shot at one of them," Bolan continued to whisper. "So you take him out while I go to work on the dock. The other one—" he started to say.

"He'll show himself soon enough," Wilson whispered back.

Bolan knew what the man meant. As soon as Wilson fired, the second sniper across the inlet would get a lock on his position. And the third one, above them—he was anybody's guess.

"Then let's do it," the Executioner said. He rose from behind the boulder, aimed his rifle at the man with the Uzi on the far end of the dock and cut loose with a 3-round burst.

The trio of .223 rounds that hit the gunman in the chest killed him long before he fell off the dock into the water.

By then Bolan had swung his M-16 to the right, sending another 3-round burst into the throat of the second of the four men with the Uzis. As a river of crimson blew from the man's neck, he heard a lone explosion from where Wilson was hiding a few yards away.

Across the inlet, high in the rocks, a rifle began tumbling down the mountain. It was followed immediately by a body.

But a second after that, another single explosion sounded from the general area where Bolan had seen the second mirror flash. The round cut through the leaves toward the spot where Wilson had hidden. Bolan could only hope the man had moved as soon as he'd fired.

The Executioner had no time to wonder, as the other two men with the submachine guns turned their weapons his way, blasting out full-auto 9 mms rounds that forced him back down behind the boulder. Bolan waited until the gunfire had stopped, then rose over the rocky barrier again. A third burst of .223s took the Uzi-man second from the right. And a final trio of rounds caught the last subgun bearer as he attempted to change magazines.

All four of the men with the Uzis had fallen off the dock, turning the murky brown water within the inlet darker with blood. Suddenly, Gomez-Garcia and his lieutenants were left standing alone on the wet wood.

The men had drawn their side arms and now Bolan turned his attention to them. As he sent another 3-round burst into the man to Gomez-Garcia's left, he heard another single round fired from the trees a few yards from where Wilson had been earlier. Good, he thought, as one of the terrorist lieutenants did a back flip into the water. The retired Texas Ranger *had* moved. And the second sniper had missed him.

But as Bolan swung his rifle to the other pistoleer, the second sniper fired again, correcting his aim to shoot at Wilson's new position.

As Bolan fired on the FARC lieutenant on Gomez-Garcia's other side, the leader of the 28th Front took off running. Jumping off the side of the dock, he began sloshing along the muddy bank next to the water.

Bolan swung his rifle toward the stumbling man as the lieutenant fell. Gomez-Garcia had one hand on his machete as he ran. But he had yet to draw his weapon, let alone to pick up one of his dead men's firearms and join the fight.

It was obvious to the Executioner that Carlos Gomez-Garcia was a murderer, not a fighter. He relied on his men for his own personal protection. And the eighty-nine men who had given their lives for his name had undoubtedly been helpless when he'd murdered them.

But the men on board the yacht were cut from a different cloth and, in the few seconds since the opening rounds had been fired, they had overcome their shock and began firing blindly at the shore. It was obvious to Bolan that they had not pinpointed either his, or Wilson's, positions. Their rounds seemed to go in every direction, ricocheting harmlessly off the mountainside.

Wilson fired another round, and Bolan saw dust and

pebbles fly into the air on the side of the mountain across the inlet. An answering round again drilled into the jungle growth around the former blacksuit. But Bolan had a fix on the second sniper himself. Flipping his M-16 to single shot, he positioned the front and rear sights on the reflection of a rifle scope he could see in the rocks above. The man behind the scope was hidden in the shadows. But by following the angle of the scope—and taking the chance that the man was right-handed—the Executioner corrected his aim. Slowly, he squeezed the trigger, letting the recoil surprise him when the striker finally fell on the round's primer. The .223 caliber hollowpoint round blasted from the rifle and found its mark.

Another rifle came sliding down the side of the mountain. The man who had held it stood up, in full view.

Before Bolan could fire again another weapon exploded from the position Wilson had been in at the beginning of the gunfight. The retired Texas Ranger's .223 had to have struck the second sniper squarely in the chest, because it drove him into the rocks, out of sight.

Bolan looked to see Gomez-Garcia still slipping and sliding frantically through the mud along the shoreline.

Moving quickly from behind the boulder, the Executioner dived into the foliage where Wilson was hidden, and heard the roar of another high-powered rifle from overhead. The heavy bullet missed his right arm by millimeters—so close that the Executioner felt the heat of the round through his blacksuit. He landed on his belly on the soggy ground and rolled to his right as a second bullet drilled into the earth a step behind him.

"We've got problems with that guy," Wilson said as

Bolan rolled into view. "Of course that very well could be the understatement of the millennium."

"You stay here," Bolan said. "See if you can get a fix on his position."

"Oh, I *know* his position," Wilson said. "He isn't nearly as high up as the guys across the way." He nodded toward the mountain on the other side of the inlet. "In fact, I *saw* him when he shot at you a second ago. The problem is, I can't get into position to shoot at him without exposing myself."

Bolan nodded. "Just stay put and wait, then," he said. "I'm going to try to stay under him, against the rocks, while I go after Pepe." He paused, ejected the partially spent magazine from his rifle and inserted a full one from a pocket in his blacksuit. "He may get a shot at me. If he does, he'll have to expose himself and he'll be yours."

Wilson frowned. "You sure you want to do that?" he asked.

"No," the Executioner said, looking at the other man. "I'm pretty sure I don't want to. But I don't see any way around it. I'm not letting Pepe get away."

"Don't forget the guys on the yacht," Wilson said. "They'll have a clear shot at you from the other side."

Bolan looked out through the leaves. By now the boat had drifted farther away, and the firing had slowed. It appeared that, like their leader now slipping through the mud, the men on the yacht were more interested in getting away now than killing him and Wilson. Bolan remembered the old ranch hand back at the house, and the other employees who couldn't believe that Bolan and Wilson were the only two men on this op. The men on the boat would likely think the same way—believing a whole squadron of police or military had been positioned there, waiting to kill them.

"I don't think the boat's a problem," the Executioner said. Then, without waiting for an answer, he dived back out of the foliage and rolled up against the side of the mountain. No gunfire erupted from over his head.

The Executioner crouched low as he made his way behind the boulder he'd used for cover earlier and then along the rocky wall of the mountain. He could see flashes of Gomez-Garcia, two hundred yards or so in the distance, still rising and falling along the edge of the water. He could have taken up a position and shot the man. But tall grass and other vegetation grew out from the shoreline, and the FARC leader was never visible for more than a split second.

Bolan knew that even a marksman of his caliber could not position his sights and fire accurately under such conditions. Somehow, he would have to get closer. And he'd have to do it without exposing himself to the sniper fire waiting above him.

The yacht could be clearly seen now, and he noted that it had turned and was heading for the entrance to the river. No more shots came from the fleeing craft. But Bolan reminded himself that it carried men as evil as the one he now stalked. Men who needed to be stopped.

Men he had no intention of letting get away.

The wall of the mountain was anything but flat and each time he was forced farther out toward the water, Bolan wondered if he might be in the sniper's field of fire. But no more rounds exploded above his head, and he continued his vigil on the clumsy FARC man as he moved on. The gap between them was closing slowly but surely as, even under the threat from above, the

Executioner made better time than the cowardly murderer who kept stomping frantically through the mud.

Suddenly, two shots rang out behind Bolan—so close together they sounded almost like one. Bolan turned in time to see that Wilson had moved out of the trees, almost to the dock. The retired Texas Ranger was on his knees. His M-16 had fallen to the ground. A second later, the man in the blacksuit fell down.

A second after that, the sniper who had been directly above them came tumbling down out of the rocks. He landed on his head, just to the side of the boulder where Bolan had hidden. The Executioner could see the fall had killed the man.

He turned back to see that Gomez-Garcia was still slipping up and down along the muddy shore. But the man had tired, and he was making little progress. Without the threat from overhead, he would be easy to catch. But Bolan couldn't go after him quite yet. He had more immediate problems to solve.

First, Wilson needed to be checked, and if the man was still alive, given whatever first aid the Executioner could render. And second, the yacht would soon be out of range of the weapon he'd lugged along from the Learjet.

Bolan left the mountainside and hurried down to the flatter land along the shore. He sprinted to where Wilson lay on the ground, rolled the man over and looked at his wound. The sniper's round had caught him in the center of the thigh, breaking the bone. But it had missed the artery running along the inside of his leg.

Wilson's eyes were open. "I'm okay," he said, trying to force a grin. "It hurts like hell, but I'm okay." He paused, winced in pain for a minute, then added, "I'll stuff some grass in the hole to stop the bleeding for now. Go get that son of a bitch and the other bastards on the boat."

Bolan nodded and hurried behind the boulder again, leaping over the dead sniper as he ran. Lifting the LAR—Land to Air Rocket launcher he'd taken from the stores on the Learjet, he aimed it at the boat nearing the exit to the inlet. He had only seconds before the yacht disappeared into the river, as he raised the LAR's sights and took a bead on the distant craft.

A moment later, the rocket flew through the air. A second after that, bright red flames leaped from the fleeing craft. The sound of the explosion echoed across the water to bounce off the sides of the mountain.

The yacht burned as Bolan dropped the handheld rocket launcher and began running along the shore. By the time he reached Gomez-Garcia, the man had run out of muscle power and was sitting on the bank staring at the fire. He turned Bolan's way when he heard the Executioner's footsteps. Then, standing up with his last ounce of energy, he drew the machete and raised it over his head.

Bolan raised the barrel of his M-16 as the terrorist–drug runner's arm came forward. He shot from the hip, letting a single .223 drill through Pepe 89's heart as the man released the machete from his hand and the weapon sailed, end-over-end toward the Executioner's head.

Bolan spun away and the machete flipped harmlessly past his face to embed itself in the muddy bank.

The Executioner walked slowly forward, knelt and jabbed a finger into Gomez-Garcia's neck. There was no pulse. Pepe 89 was dead. The mission was finished.

Almost.

IT WOULD BE A LITTLE crowded on the Learjet but they could all fly back together. Bolan, Wilson, and the men of Phoenix Force. Besides, the Executioner thought, as he opened the back door of Carlos Gomez-Garcia's Cadillac, the retired Texas Ranger could use the medical aid Phoenix Force's Calvin James would provide. The former Navy SEAL medic would keep the thigh wound in check until Wilson was back in the U.S.

Reaching inside the car, Bolan took one of the injured man's arms and helped him out of the back seat. He supported Wilson's weight as they made their way to where Grimaldi had landed the Learjet on the ranch's landing strip.

A minute later, they were in the air and on their way back to Bogotá. The Executioner got Wilson positioned on a cot bolted to the wall in the rear of the plane, pulled a hypodermic needle and vial of morphine from the medical kit on board, then gave the man a shot over all of his protests. His eyes closed in mid-sentence and he was out.

Bolan took a seat next to Grimaldi and strapped himself in. Pulling the cell phone from his blacksuit, he tapped in the number that David McCarter was using. A moment later the familiar British accent said, "Hello, Striker."

"How fast can you get to the Bogotá airport?" Bolan asked the man.

"We're roughly two hours out," he said. "Ready to go home?"

"Almost," the Executioner said.

"We'll head that way immediately," McCarter said. "But what about Captain Guttierez?"

"He still sleeping?" the Executioner asked.

"That's affirmative."

"Rent a hotel room somewhere close to the police

station. Leave him there and leave him a note telling him that Ramon Marquez ordered the hit on Pepe 89. That should take care of Marquez. If the CNP don't get him, his fellow FARC members will."

Bolan thought about the many drug dealers, murderers and corrupt politicians and officials who were destroying Colombia. He knew the president had his work cut out for him.

And the Executioner knew he'd be back again to help even the score.

James Axler
Outlanders®

CLOSING THE COSMIC EYE

Rumors of an ancient doomsday device come to the attention of the Cerberus rebels when it's stolen by an old enemy, Gilgamesh Bates. The pre-Dark mogul who engineered his own survival has now set his sights on a controlling share of the cosmic pie. Kane, Grant, Brigid and Domi ally themselves with Bates's retired personal army, a time-trawled force of American commandos ready to take the battle back to Bates himself, wherever he's hiding in the galaxy, before the entire universe disappears in the blink of an eye.

Available February 2007 wherever books are sold.